To: Wandg chope you
enjoy your Journey at
the call center and
this book helps!

Kusta'ma Kare

OLHALLEY

To order additional copies of this book, contact:

Xlibris Corporation

1-888-795-4274

www.Xlibris.com

Orders@Xlibris.com

36780

Contents

Acknowledgments

To TG. I thank you so very much for the opportunity. It was your intuitiveness, that people with the desire to change can do so if given the opportunity. If Webster himself had known you, he would have created another word for *awesome*; the word in comparison to you is truly an understatement. To all my managers over the years who knew beyond doubt that my mind and body were not always in the same domicile, I thank you. There are a host of friends who had to endure with my insanity during my publication process thanks to all. To friends and family who supported my endeavor, pushing and cheering me forward, your support gave me the strength and courage to continue. Thanks for all the phones calls and e-mails accepted and received on my behalf to see this venture through. Daughter, I love you (R/D). To my Pudding (Mom), thank you for the day you could not rest until you found me seven years ago. I have not looked back. To my sponsor T, thanks for helping me save myself. And a moment of silence for the addict who still suffers.

To those out there who started a project and did not finish, to those out there that have a dream but are afraid to pursue it, this one is for you.

-olhalley

The only thing one does not see through is the very thing one does not do.

Fear is premeditated failure.

Finishing takes unprecedented courage.

-olhalley

Author's Notes

I WOULD LIKE to begin by stating *Kusta'ma Kare* was written with the sole purpose of bringing enjoyment to the pleasure of reading. To heighten human awareness for human kindness in a world where we have taken so many things for granted, such as the good morning at the start of another day, failing to realize something as simple as a kind gesture, the lack of which can make or break one's day.

Whatever your nationality, gender, generation, or financial status maybe, *Kusta'ma Kare* was written to traverse all of life's barriers.

My sincere desire is that you will discover *Kusta'ma Kare* an enjoyable read in the content that it was intended.

To take into account a thought that you never before pondered, and possibly finding room for change within one self if change is needed or desired.

Kusta'ma Kare is a fictional story, but all the contents of *Kusta'ma Kare* do not have to remain part of a fictional story. Kusta'ma Kare has the capability and potential to become a reality! If everyone would make an attempt to Customer Care, everyone everyday . . . Enjoy the journey my character takes in an attempt to live life, and transform the lives of others, the Kusta'ma Kare way. The journey begins . . .

...The journey

How Did I Get Here?

As I ROSE from my white Lane sofa, I stopped for a brief moment glancing about my attractive dwelling in total admiration of how my life had changed in ten short years. As I reflect on years past, it seemed not so incredibly long ago—walking to work in Payless Shoes to a famous pizzeria restaurant, to this moment where I am in awe of my life. I looked over my beautiful residence on one of the breathtaking Hawaiian Islands.

As I walked toward the balcony, the sliding glass door was slightly ajar. Sliding it completely open, I stopped and took a deep lungful of ocean air. I continued outside, appreciating the view of the palm trees gently swaying in the warm summer breeze.

Linda, I asked myself, how does one go from serving pizza to here? I am the CEO (and for those of you who are acronym impaired, chief executive officer) of the largest customer care center in the world. The sole proprietor of a conglomerate named Kusta'ma Kare. Kusta'ma Kare is a customer services center of various services from communication, energy, and water supply to major cities and majority of rural areas in the United States, a business I sold only two weeks previously after ten years of determination, struggles, and fun. Was everything I endured through the years worth it? Yes. With all the catastrophic calamities, and the near destruction, it took momentous strength to overcome some of the adversities. That's why Kusta'ma Kare is the global icon that it is today.

My name is Linda Morehouse. I am a strong-minded, self-motivated woman who got a sluggish start at living life. I take into account each step of the events in my life that led to this day of reckoning and the journey it took to get here.

I remember one day a little over ten years ago when I was taking a call from a customer. I could not accept as true when people dial that 1-800 number how they seem to forget that another human being is on the other side of the line. Worse yet is when the person who answers that same 1-800 number forgets that they're talking to another human being. Somehow we as people have misplaced compassion for one another. Customers abusing customer service representatives and customer service representatives abusing customers. If you have not yet surmised, I used to be a customer service operator . . . Well my journey begins there.

Ten years earlier:

I lived in an extremely small town where the population was less than twenty thousand inhabitants. In the town I reside you do not have to travel far to view cows off the side of the road gnawing on grass. There was the stench of onions growing from a nearby field when you awake first thing in the morning on a scorching summer day. I am still uncertain just how I ended up here, or even why I remained. I used to reside in one of the major metropolitan cities—you know, the ones with one-hundred-plus-story buildings. Cities with elevators, escalators, cabs, limousines, and smog—you know, the good life. Well if you do not live in one of these major cities, just watch a movie, and if you live a few miles from one, maybe you can follow my dismay at my current living conditions. This particular small town which I live in does not have a structure over two stories high. I assess so the crop-dusting planes can fly by crop dusting. Now that you have a visual of my living status in life, I can continue.

I lived in a tiny apartment overlooking nothing but another tiny apartment for the most part somewhat content. I have however become contented with the fact that somehow this was not how my life was to exist.

At this moment in my life I work at a famous pizzeria. As a midday buffet server, I was the best. Walking home one day from servicing customer's pizza, I thought to myself I don't remember my prayer as a child to be serving pizza at this age. But whatever, I looked up at the clouds setting low and gray as moisture brazed my face. I contemplated; will I make it to my tiny apartment before it rains? I was not quite forty years of age, and something just did not feel right. I recognize that I cannot serve up pizza until I'm sixty years of age. The reason that I am serving pizza at my current age is another story in itself. My point and my realization at this age is that I cannot continue on this path.

I attempted to put my life back together again, not that it was all together to begin with, after tripping over numerous pitfalls that one can fall in, in life. If there was a solitary pitfall out there in the pitfalls of life, I would surely discover it. So I prayed to God, "Father, at my age I could do with a sit-down job and more money. How am I ever to put my life back together at these wages?" I looked down at my check one day literally crying, wondering how I was to rise above my current living conditions.

I was not fortunate to learn most things that others had learned, should know, or at least have experienced at my age. You know, simple things like typing. Due to the computer age, most people should already know how, and these days most learn it while they are in kindergarten. Nor did I achieve a degree in mathematics. I always felt that I was destined for great things. I just felt it in my bones, but how does one go from serving pizza to greatness? At this point, I was clueless.

After work, some days I would take my tips and squander a couple of dollars on state lottery tickets. Some nights, I would even go to sleep and dream that I won the Million Dollar State Lottery, only to be painfully awakened by the alarm clock reminding me it is time to wake up and serve pizza again. Fully awake and rubbing my eyes thinking, darn it, you mean, I did not win the state lottery for one hundred zillion dollars?

I prepared for work, still in shock that I am still poor, and wondered why I am never the winner. When I heard the lottery results on television, I was saddened knowing someone, somewhere, is holding the winning lottery numbers that I omitted by one number to the left or to the right. They picked six, and I picked seven, wouldn't you know it.

At this point, I have reasoned that some fortunes will be won, while other fortunes will have to be made. Depends on the fortune you are seeking, I guess. Some fortunes are found in love. You can be one of fortune and not be fortunate enough to find true love. You know, the couples that one might see kissing in the car next to you at the red light. If you're single, this sight may make you want to cry your eyes out. They may or may not have a dime but were fortunate enough to find fortune in true love. Other fortunes are found in the fulfillment of one's profession, someone like a doctor, teacher, or a priest, for instance. I guess I will have to define within myself what good fortune means to me.

Maybe that is the key word, "good fortune," and not just fortune. What a concept! I have learned that one cannot seek for something if they do not know what they are seeking for. It's like waking up in the morning, getting dressed preparing to leave your home, grasping your car keys to take a drive, but having no destination in mind. What's the point of starting the ignition without a destination in mind? Pointless, I think?

Well time passed, as time does. I was still walking to work in Payless Shoes, making maybe ten cents more than I did last year; I may be ready to buy a Mercedes! I am doing a little better, still serving pizza, but able to save a few tips every now and then to maybe one day, buy a car. I purchased a little car for two thousand dollars cash, from a coworker's mom. She allowed me to pay five hundred in down payment and five hundred a month thereafter. I was so excited that I did not realize that I literally had to sit on the ground to get in my car door. My little car was so low to the ground that when passing two-way traffic at night, the oncoming headlights blinded me, but I would just say at least I'm not walking. When you compare what you have now to then, you tend to be grateful when blinding lights bear down on you. Now equipped with transportation, I decided to venture out—employment wise, that is.

I was constantly viewing the help wanted ads for better employment. Overqualified, under qualified, at least five or more years experience. I could just see the candidate for presidency of the United States filling out an application for the president, with Congress or whoever saying your years of experience did not qualify for the position of president! I do not know why some jobs require experience; they are only going to retrain you their way anyway. Rocket scientist I could see, auto mechanic or brain surgeon maybe. But I was not seeking this type of career choice. There has got to be something out there, a step up from serving pizza, that I can handle. Not that serving pizza is a demeaning task, just not one that I can easily accept at my age and my drive for betterment in life. I could apply for the position of cruise director on the love boat.

That's it. I can find love and employment all in one application. I checked there too, "must have cruise director experience and in case the captain gets sick, navigational skills a must." At the bottom of the application was a footnote—"navigational skills a must"! I guess I should register for online classes to be a brain surgeon; home-study course, degree by mail.

One day, while reviewing the classified ads for sit-down employment, I saw "Wanted Customer Care Representative" at a popular cellular company. I contemplated to myself for about one second, "Hey! What's to consider? The opportunity to sit down all day and talk to people. This would be perfect; I would not have to be taught a thing". I learned to talk as soon as I was two years of age and have not shut up since. This would be prefect!

As faith would have it after testing my speaking skills I guess, and an interview to see if I had hands to type, I'll get the job. I expressed my gratitude to God that its location was only two miles from where I lived. I presume my car will get me there and back.

The people working at this particular call center were from all walks of life. As nice as everyone seemed, I still felt this is not the place my life would find permanency in way of career choices. There were only very few people wearing blue suits, with starched white shirts, carrying animal skin briefcases. There were no women with hundred-dollar hairstyles, which was great because I would not have fit in. Somewhere in one of those pitfalls, I lost my desire to dress fashionably.

I guess that was one of the reasons why the only experience I needed was the experience of speech, working arms, and fingers to type. With cows grazing not three miles from where reside, what else can I expect? There were some people who, indeed were very nicely dressed, and had a very professional manner; and for the life of me, I still could not motivate myself to do the same. Either way, dressed fancy or not, I have to say that a lot of true friendships spawned. I am found out that when you spend more time at work than home; your coworkers become your brother, sisters, at times mom and dad. Most were so smart that I often wonder why they are here. The job requirement for this position, I obtained with limited skills. You know, the walking, talking skills that every employer out there was tearing my door down to have me run their company. Smart or not, I'm the best, so away to work I go!

Not losing sight of the fact that, I got just what I prayed for—to sit all day. I could have been working with un-trained orangutans, and been just as happy. Thirteen hundred odd people coming and going at all hours of the day comprises the call center where I am now employed. Oh happy day!

The first few months was training, training, and more training. Why do I have to be trained so much? I know how to talk! Then again, looking around the room, I felt training was a must. There were teenagers right out of high school, and employees with Mohawks, and tattoos. You cannot expect Mercedes performance from a Volkswagen. But with that mentality, as an interviewer I would not have been hired. I don't think I'm even a Volkswagen.

Training was a must. I did not know how many versions of the English language there were, until I attempted to communicate with some of my new coworkers. I communicated with them more often than not. I found myself asking the Mohawk kid for help every day. Never judge a book by the cover. My instructor was the most delightful and intelligent person. I wonder most times why they did not choose to be a lawyer or doctor, and why their career path did not take on a different direction. Had it not been for my instructor being so patient with my mental disabilities the below journey would have never unfolded. I also found out that when I had to remember more than olives on a pizza, I had a form of retention problem. I heard everything my instructor taught, but for the life of me without four thousand posted notes everywhere most time by the end of the day I could not remember a thing. None the less my instructor continued encouragement for me to remain. I do believe that people are placed in our lives for reasons and seasons.

After weeks and weeks of customer care training on how not to abuse a customer, I learned that the customer is always right. After about sixty days of taking calls from these always-right customers, I often wondered to myself why this training was not also given to the customers because they're the ones that were being abusive as well. This in turn turned good customer care representatives bad. "Give me this, get me that. I will not pay this bill, and matter of fact, let me speak to your manager!"

"Ma'am," I would say, "I am sorry that your phone does not work in Zimbabwe."

"Ma'am, may I ask, can you use your phone in most of your home area?"

At that point, the customer exclaimed, "I'm not at home right now! I will be here for two weeks, and if I am unable to use my phone, what is your point?" She continued, "I should not have to pay for service if I cannot use my phone when I am out in the middle of nowhere. If you cannot or will not adjust my account for two weeks of service lost, I'll just go to another company that will . . ." Boy, was that ever an open-ended statement. Most times, when that statement was made, I would want to hit the cancel button right then and end the call in midsentence.

If the customer didn't pay her bill, her phone would surely cease to work. If Superman had that attitude when he could not locate a phone booth to transform from Clark Kent, no one would have been saved. I can just picture a falling meteor and Clark Kent running around looking for a phone booth that he can't find saying, "Well I guess the planet won't be saved today; I cannot locate a phone booth." No, Superman would just use what he had. No problem, he would say, I see one of those; stick your head in the box phones, I'll change there . . . up, up, and away! Planet saved because he used what he had. Thank God for Superman.

What I wanted to share with this customer now in Zimbabwe is that I went on a cruise for two weeks and did not live in my house. However, I did not call the cable company and say I did not have my television on for two weeks. Do I still have to pay the whole monthly service? If my television is broken and I was unable to watch cable I should not pay.

Then there was the customer who constantly complains or disputes paying a bill based on an underage child who ran up the phone bill and now they have to mortgage their home. They would say to me, "Miss, you do not understand I have to know where little Johnny is at all times." When I was a minor, my mom took me everywhere I went and always communicated with the parent of the house that I was to visit. When I was young, there was no such thing as sending a child out in the world with a cell phone to call and tell a parent where they are. You better have an agenda when you leave home of where you are going, leave the contact number on the kitchen counter, and be back by eight o'clock. I now know why some children have to be sent to boot camp for disciplinary behaviors, children in court divorcing their parents. Ha! Take little Johnny where he has to go, Mama, and you will know where he is.

Well of course, due to excellent training, I could not say this to this customer. So of course, I attempted to reach a manager to inform him or her of my customer's concerns. "Get a call back!" the manager would reply. I went back on the phone again to get called a few things that my mom did not name me. I searched my memory to see if, at any time, I signed a contract that stated I gave up my rights to be treated or talked to like a human being. I wanted to help people, but they don't want help; they just want everything for free. This customer care position gave a true meaning to the cliché "give a person an inch and they will take a mile." That's what I can do, open a school not for customer service training but for customer training. (Class says, "Yes, you can help me, and thank you very much." Very good customers. Class dismissed.)

What would sadden me even more are certain days when I go to break or lunch passing desks along the way and hearing a customer service representative being rude or condescending with a customer? Is it so very hard just to be kind? The same information shared can have a different meaning just in the delivery of the information from either party. A broken phone is still a broken phone, mad or glad. I cannot restore your service without payment. The information is the same, mad or glad. What are we as people so mad about that the smallest trigger turns us from glad to mad in a split second sometime less? It is like being rude is first nature, and kindness second or a low third in priorities.

Some days it would be more than I could tolerate. With the personality I have always laughing and finding the lighter side of life, most of the time it was hard not to laugh at some of their concerns. Whatever happened to world hunger, our rising crime rate, and terrorism? It appeared that a missed call or the failing to make a call is their only concern. What does that say about them as an individual and about mankind itself? One customer had the audacity to enlighten me they lost a million dollar deal when they engaged in conversation with a party in China and right in the middle of negotiations lost the connection! I thought to myself, why would any sane person make a million dollar deal by relying on something as unreliable as a cellular telephone? One would think those types of deals should be made on a landline phone or a satellite phone with better connectivity.

I would wonder about such thoughts to myself day to day as I listen to calls. Doing my best to soothe the customer; I am still filled with disbelief. It was a character-building job, to say the least. If I did not arrive with strong character, I unquestionably will leave with some.

Well I got what I prayed for, a job where I could sit all day and talk, and talk, and talk, sometimes reasoning into people that a lost call is not a loss of life! Get a grip! Being on the other side of the fence and having to place calls from time to time to a different 800 number, I paid close attention to be as kind as possible regardless of what my issue was about or how upsetting it was. Then to get a customer service representative that was just downright rude and paying absolutely no attention to me or my needs, I just don't get it! Maybe I am the one that's being too nice? No, that's not it; people have forgotten to be nice. I am further finding rather people are taking the call or making the call; sometimes it just doesn't matter that lack of kindness has fallen all around me. Are there too many people on the planet earth? Do we need to move some people around to another planet? People would be screaming, "take me back to earth! I'll be nice."

How very hard is it to be nice (not syrupy, just pleasant) to one another and realize that our task is to find resolution and offer resolution, whether listening to the problem or delivering the problem. I don't know, but one would think if one had an issue and it was in the power of the other person on the other end of the line to help find resolution, I would be as pleasant as possible. One should also consider that if it takes a million customers to support a company so I can get a pay increase and live a decent lifestyle, then it is my obligation to keep generating revenue for my company; one would be as pleasant as possible. You would think? Time to go back to work—I think too much.

Thinking for me was hard with my brain an absentee member of my body most of the time. So where does all this thinking come from? I believe this kind of thinking comes from my heart, more like a feeling than a thought, just how I feel we should treat one another.

Time passed by, and with that, my salary has increased. I am dressing a little better. I cannot afford to shop at the local stores that carried someone else's name on the tag instead of their own. My income still has not permitted me such luxuries as shopping at Macy's or Nordstrom—nonetheless, I try to keep up with the working class in this town, but that look they have of living down the street away from the cows is hard to achieve. After a while, I got comfortable with that look and worked hard at trying to achieve it. What is happening to me? I feel like a fish out of water. Try picturing a fish in a birdcage feeling at home with the bird still in the cage! That's how I felt at times.

From time to time, in my stillness, I experienced the eerie feeling creeping up the back of my neck that this is still not the life intended for me. It was like my mind was watching my life from afar waiting for my body to catch up to where it was. Two entities dwelling in one domain, unsure of the other's destiny. It was strictly torture waiting for mind and body to become one. I would wonder why I'd daydream so often and see myself living the lifestyle of the rich and famous or making a contribution to world change. At other times, I would find myself trying to have a thought but could not because I could not connect with my inner self/mind and body not in sync. My body was going a hundred miles an hour to grab hold of my mind running a gauntlet. Living an out-of-body experience, waiting to get where I was going was challenging. With my mind watching me from a distance, waving me forward and not to sit down for long, this is not the life I intended for us. Get up and stop singing that jingle!

While in this dormant state of life, I would sometimes be contented that this is my destiny, reporting to work on top of the world. I actually caught myself, singing a jingle " ♫ I was born to be a customer service rep ♫ !" Stop, what am I singing? A person can be brainwashed on many levels, and putting limitations on oneself just by their mind-set. Scary thought. I found that I was not born to be a customer service representative, but possibly born to train them. Feels like another song coming on. I guess to train a customer care representative, you have to had been one at one time, or at least be born with the mind-set to execute it.

The skill set for the customer service ad was most deceiving though. I thought all my job description entailed talking. As it turned out, I typed all day and kept a calculator on my desktop at all times. I had to learn how to troubleshoot cellular telephones. I had to learn where the signal comes from and ends for a call to connect. Why did I need to learn these things? I was not going out there to fix one cell site if it ceased to work. Funny, for all the things I had to learn, I should have earned a degree in telecommunications technical support and installation instead of a paycheck to answer the phones, or a paycheck for both.

I am still grateful for life, employment, and the opportunity to sit all day. I continued on this path wondering how much more abuse I would endure before one day I completely lost touch with reality and shared with a customer what I really thought about their trivia issues related to a cell phone, but I didn't and couldn't not bring my character to do so.

Mr. Jacobs

After overcoming the majority of pitfalls in life, I was still waiting to catch up with myself or with where my mind was taking me. I had become such an optimist about life; you know, my glass-half-full syndrome, walking through life with rose-colored glasses on. I continued to provide the best that I could muster up. I received numerous awards for an outstanding customer service representative. Give your best in life, I say, no matter what your task in life is. As you will discover later, thank God that I did because on this particular day, the heavens opened when my headset lit up indicating an incoming caller.

"Thank you for calling . . . my name is Linda Morehouse how may I provide you with excellent customer service today?"

"Good morning, Linda, and how are you doing today?" a customer replied in a tone that I do not often hear after I clock in to work.

"Wonderful, thank you, sir, for asking, and how is your day going?"

"Not too well, Linda, at the moment. My name is James R. Jacobs III, and something has caused my cell phone to cease working. My assistant Barbara usually attends to these matters, and she is not present today unfortunately for me to advise her of my situation."

I made small talk with Mr. Jacobs while I reviewed his account attempting to locate the problem. He really was a joy to speak with and made me smile. His way with words and his patience made my heart light. I felt like singing my jingle " ♪ I was born to be a customer service rep! ♪ " It was something about his voice and tone that was regal, like he was better than most but at the same time did not have a hint of arrogance.

Further into the call, the source of his nonworking cell phone had been discovered. Mr. Jacobs's account had been provisioned to be debited from his corporate credit card account on a monthly basis which had expired. With the company credit card not being updated, the account had become delinquent and suspended for nonpayment. "Mr. Jacobs, I have located the source for your nonworking phone, and if you would allow me just one moment, I will temporarily restore your services." I went on with the business of being a customer service representative and also inquired as to when his assistant could possibly call in and update their credit card information. He advised me by the end of the week she should be returning to the office. And if not, he would call in the information himself. Mr. Jacobs asked if I had an extension or if anyone could update his credit card information. I advised that anyone can address their concerns, and update his account.

None of the information I shared with him got him unnerved or changed his tone which further confirmed that the gentleman had a mannerism to be admired. He was immune to pettiness. It was a small matter that could be resolved. His only goal for the call was to be able to use his cell phone and was genuinely glad at the end of our nine-minute call that he was able to do so. I could also tell that Mr. Jacobs was a man of power; on what level, I had no idea. His phone number was only one of hundreds of phones on the account. The balance on this account was more than I made in three years' wages. Nonetheless, he was not discourteous like most people in his position could have been. I thought to myself, with more people like him calling in, I would come to work early and work late.

Mr. Jacobs thanked me numerous times, stating that I was most helpful and kind and he wished that more people in my field were as kind and helpful; he went on and on. I thanked Mr. Jacobs for the kind words and also assured him that with his demeanor, it was my pleasure and not a task to assist him. At the end of that nine-minute call, I sung my jingle " ♫ I was born to be a customer service rep. ♫ "

I gave no more thought to Mr. Jacobs as days passed except when I was being called something by a customer other than the name my parents named me. From time to time I wondered where people like Mr. Jacobs came from. Did he come from another planet? Surely he was not born on this planet or even a neighboring one. He just did not sound like the kind of man that packed a ray gun. Not that I would know what someone packing a ray gun would sound like. Three weeks passed since I had the pleasure of speaking with Mr. Jacobs when twelve dozen long-stemmed red roses arrived by courier service to the call center where I was employed. One of the boxes held a handcrafted thank-you card to my company for having enough insight to hire such an attentive and caring customer service representative. I was overwhelmed to say the least. I was the envy of my workplace for a day.

I wonder just how Mr. Jacobs located me when I never gave the city or even state for that matter. I found later that when you have as much money as Mr. Jacobs, you can find out anything about anyone not just in the United States but also in the world. He probably knows what kind of car I drive, where I live, and what I like to eat. But why he would want such personal information was my next question. Was he a stalker, millionaire murderer? What is this, flowers first, death next? Nah, he didn't seem that type either, but neither did Ted Bundy. Mr. Jacobs you gave me such optimism for mankind. I believed . . . and now you may turn out to be a possible stalker, possible murderer. There was no jingle at the end of that thought.

I pushed back all thoughts of evilness and conspiracy to the back of my mind, which was hard to do when your mind and body are not of one entity. I put that thought in an envelope and made note to myself when my mind does show up to share that information with them.

Three years have now passed since I began working at the call center. I bought a different car that I only have to bend down instead of get on the ground to get in. The car lot was one of those buy-here, pay-your-car-note-here car lots. Boy, you never want that payment to get lost in the mail. So I painfully drove forty-five minutes down the highway every month to hand-deliver my monthly payment.

Going to work every day in my updated car still plagued with that eerie feeling crawling up the back of my neck that this job was not where my fortune lay, but I carried on singing my jingle, periodically keeping up my momentum.

During a three-year span, I found that some of the friendships that developed were also having out-of-body experiences. Wanting a better way of life but somehow stuck not knowing how to come up from underneath, I would walk by their desk and see them like myself, daydreaming in between calls. I could not or did not want to get comfortable with the living paycheck-to-paycheck mentality. I did not really know why, but in the back of my mind, I mingled less with those that felt this job was the answer to their prayers; and if this job was their answer, then this is the job for them.

I guess that's fine when your mind and body are one, and your mind is not constantly pulling you in another direction. There is nothing wrong when one finds their niche in life. For me, this was not the case. I guess everyone has to be something in life, but I felt this is not the something that was meant for my life! This was just not the something I was born for, regardless of what my current theme song says. I was ready to stop life from happening to me, and start happening to life! Waiting to find out what that something is going to be for me, I pushed forward. My mind defiantly had another destiny for my body, or my mind would not be in such turmoil and a constant absentee member of my body most times.

After three and a half years of taking calls, a letter arrives at my apartment. I looked down at the return address, and it was from an attorney's office. My God, what have I done now! I thought I was doing fairly well avoiding the pitfalls in life. The envelope was a very expensive one, and the embossed calligraphy was most impressive requesting my presence in New York City, for a matter that concerned Mr. Jacobs R. III. I searched my mind; that is still somewhere in the future, I thought, trying to remember the call that day. Did I do anything that was not up to conduct becoming of a customer service representative?

Along with the letter was the time and date of my departure at a private airstrip and hotel accommodations at a five-star hotel. The date was set for two weeks from the postmark date. As I can remember I did not do anything unethical that would require me to be in attendance with an attorney. Was I being sued for something? If that was the case, the company that I worked for would have notified me, and not the person I had contact with personally. If I was being sued, I do not believe a private jet would be provided.

Panic filled my mind, which did me no good, because again, I had to remember my mind did not reside in my body at this present time. My body went limp waiting for a signal from my brain as far as what to do. I felt at times, my brain was a coward for letting my body experience all these things alone. Then again, if not for my mind having a different vision of what my life should be, I would have ceased moving forward long ago. Just what my mind had in store for me, I had no idea. It was like my mind knew my future and did not want me to lie down until I got there. I guess that's where the cliché came from, that where the mind goes, the body will follow.

Sitting at my kitchen table, I reached behind me for the wall phone. I dialed the number beneath the attorney's name on the business card. The attorney's name on the card, Bernard Willingham, had a string acronym behind his name indicating his status in life. My hands shook as I dialed the number. I hung up twice. Finally getting enough courage to allow a ring through without hanging up, I asked, "May I speak to Mr. Willingham please." A gentle but powerful voice answered the phone.

"This is Mr. Willingham, may I help you," Bernard said.

"My name is Linda Morehouse. I received a letter from your law firm requesting my present in New York, may I ask in what regards is my presence required?"

Mr. Willingham assured me no ill faith had befallen me. He did not advise me why my presence was required, only that it was imperative that I attend the meeting. I asked if Mr. Jacobs would be attending this meeting; I was only informed that more would be revealed at the scheduled meeting time. I was also informed that any wages lost as a result of my taking time off work would be more than compensated.

I requested two weeks off work to prepare for my trip. I figured as long as I was being compensated, nothing would go unpaid. I needed a whole week to pull myself together and another week to decide what to do, where to go, and whom to inform that I am going out of town for a meeting just in case there is a ray gun. I barely got any sleep the entire two weeks that I was off work. My constant thought now was that this was yet another pitfall, and this came with my head up and eyes open.

My mind did a cameo appearance, and over powered my body, saying go!

For two weeks I was a basket case; I did not know what to pack for my trip. I decided to go into my four hundred dollars savings account and at least buy something that did not say that I live around the corner with the cows. I purchased two pantsuits at a moderate cost and thought I would put a little more out for my shoes than I would generally spend. I only packed one medium suitcase so that in case I was kidnapped and incarcerated, the authorities would not have a lot to sort through.

What am I saying? I am losing my mind? I cannot wait until this ordeal is over. That's even crazier. My mind and body have not been in sync for years; I can't lose something that's not in my possession.

Into my second week, with three days before my flight, a phone call came informing me that a limousine would be picking me up to take me to the airport. Fear gripped every part of my body, but in spite of my fear, I continued with the travel plans. My mind actually made a cameo appearance again, twice in two weeks taunting me . . ."hurry up, get packed, stop procrastinating." Oh now you want to show up spouting orders. Where have you been the last few years of my life?

The private jet that I boarded was breathtaking, to say the least, and The most beautiful thing I had never seen in my life. There were two attendants, which looked more like French models, who saw to my boarding needs. My luggage was carried aboard and placed in a deep closet. I didn't pack much, so they did not have much to store. I dressed in a simple black knit suit with a white linen blouse and low black flats. I was escorted to my seat and made comfortable.

My seat was a large back cream leather chair with attached seat belts for flight standards. I viewed a list of movies and a menu that could have only come from my favorite television show *Lifestyles of the Rich and Famous*. I glanced over the menu and decided to order the Alaskan king crab with drawn butter, rib eye steak, a baked potato, and seltzer water garnished with lime. I settled in for a three-hour flight. At the end of the flight, I was greeted once again by a limousine. I was driven through the streets of New York, the scenic route. The limousine took me to a grand hotel, the likes of which I've never seen except on television of course. It was grand in every way. I can't really connect with what I am feeling, but my mind made another cameo appearance . . . go in the door stupid, just don't stand there with your mouth gaping opened.

The meeting was set for 9:00 a.m., which gave me, I thought, plenty of time to catch my breath and attempt to get a good night's sleep. I kept expecting word from Mr. Jacobs welcoming me, or at least to offer up an explanation of my requested presence. No word came. I went up to my room to order up dinner, due to the fact my wardrobe was not up to par for a night on the town in New York; I thought the fashion police would surely arrest me. I'm sure they rode around New York all day on bikes just waiting to arrest someone who is not politically dressed for outdoor strolling. Before going to the market, these people I'm sure visited their fashion designer first. Everything was a fashion statement. I rode up the elevator to my suite, thinking to myself that the bellboys here dress better than I did.

Much to my surprise, as I lay my coat and purse on the bed, there was an array of clothing in all styles and colors from designers all over the world. There were also boxes of shoes, Victoria's Secret to wear before adorning myself, and accessories. In the center of the room was a smorgasbord of cuisines from fruit, salads, bread, and fancy cheeses. Roses, roses, and more roses everywhere, on a small table, more roses with a card simply have a wonderful night on the town. A driver will be downstairs at your disposal and a number to call is listed below. Inside the card was one thousand dollars; now I'm really nervous . . . what is going on! The movie *Pretty Woman* came to my mind (which still was not in attendance at that moment, coward), but I'm no hooker, streetwalker, or lady of the night, body-for-hire, or whatever they're called. Once again, my body filled with fear and delight, all at the same time. Maybe Mr. Jacobs found out what my yearly wages were and felt sorry for me, and desires to adopt me? It was a possible but not likely that something this wonderful would ever happen to me.

I was too excited to eat, so I nibbled on a few bits and pieces of food and then took a luxury bubble bath and decided to enjoy the ride. Whatever event that was going to take place was going to come about, I'm here now; good or bad, whatever the outcome. I still felt like a hog right before the slaughter, being fattened up for the kill.

After my bath, I tried on a few clothes for hours, until I found what I thought was perfectly suited for the likes of New York City. If not, the fashion police would just have to give me a ticket. I viewed myself in the mirror; wow, what a transformation. Any reporters that may be in the lobby would whisper to each other why the bellboys didn't inform them someone important had arrived at the hotel tonight and camera lights would be continuously flashing. As I embarked off the elevator, there were no blinding lights.

I went on a carriage ride around Central Park, with a mink blanket for warmth and comfort. I looked at all the beautiful people walking around and shopping, going here and there. Two hours later, I was back at the hotel for a restful night sleep, and sleep I did for the first time since I can remember—without worry. The hotel phone rang, waking me, and my heart jumped. Mr. Jacobs, I thought to myself.

"Ms. Morehouse this is Bernard Willingham, did I wake you?"

"No," I said sounding a little groggy; he only wanted to inquire how my trip to New York was and if it was a pleasant one. Did I find my accommodations satisfactory? I thanked him for the wonderful accommodations and said that everything to this point was wonderful. I then asked about Mr. Jacobs. He just replied that he would see me in the morning, and told me to have a wonderful night's sleep and that he was looking forward to meeting me in the morning. I placed the phone back on cradle and stared at it for a moment. What does all this mean?

I awoke to the smell of fresh-baked croissants and coffee. I chose something a little more casual for a morning down in the lobby. I went downstairs to the mezzanine where I located a beauty salon and got the works. Pedicure, manicure, and a three-hundred-dollar full makeover. I am now prepared to face any fate that may befall me. Whatever happens now at least I'll look first-class while I'm falling apart.

It was only a thirty-minute ride from the hotel, but the hustle and bustle of this town made me feel as if it took forever. I felt that I was on another planet. No cows gnawing on grass around the corner from the hotels here, that's for sure. When we arrived, I stood outside the limousine and stared up at the building, where I was to meet my demise.

The building lured into the heavens it seemed to be endless in height. It was a one hundred and fifty story building. We took a private elevator ride to the penthouse floor. The elevator stopped. My heart pounded as the elevator doors opened to display a vast room. Its appearance was office motif but not. As I stepped off the elevator into a humungous room, a charming middle-age lady greeted me at the elevator door.

"Hello, Ms. Morehouse," she said, "my name is Barbara Willingham. It is my pleasure to finally meet you. Everyone has been eagerly awaiting your arrival."

Entering a very handsomely decorated room were six individuals awaiting my arrival. There was Barbara, the assistant to Mr. Jacobs, who inadvertently through her absence was the reason I was present here today. She and I made seven in attendance. She was the first of the six to approach me. Lovely lady, well groomed, and in her late forties, she wore her hair in a French bun with not a hair out of place. Her shoes were of moderate height for business but accented her wardrobe wonderfully. Her teeth gleamed inside a lip-lined smile, and her makeup was flawless. Barbara had a strong, sincere handshake, and her eyes met mine, as she asked, "How was your flight on the company jet?" Barbara was a self-made woman who came from money and married into money. Her marriage of twenty years was a very successful one. Barbara's husband, William, known as Bill, was leading attorney for Mr. Jacobs's various companies. Bill and Barbara shared many common interests and vacationed all over the world. They had four children: William Jr., Scott, Henry, and Sahara, who are now full adults living their own successful lives.

She was secure as a woman and wife to Bernard. I now know why Mr. Jacobs relied on her so.

"Wonderful," I replied, and much unexpected, I must say. One of the six remaining was Charles Nelson Edwards, Esq., one that I found of his many personal attorneys to be the most interesting. Mr. Edwards was a tall and handsome man; he was breathtaking, to say the least. His eyes were a warm simmering light brown but ever observing. His hair was jet black and slightly graying at his temples—more from wisdom than age, I believe. He appeared to be gliding across the room when he came toward me. Mr. Edwards looked as though he was cut from a *Gentleman's Quarterly* magazine. He smiled with piano-key perfect teeth—the white keys, that is. "Welcome, Ms. Morehouse, my name is Charles Nelson Edwards, attorney at law, close friend and associate to Mr. Jacobs. I hope that your room accommodations and limousine ride over was comfortable." (Charles, after only five years of marriage to a woman that wanted him more at home than at the office, had been divorced now over eight years.) Charles was a dedicated attorney to his client, Mr. Jacobs. Although Charles's wife had everything she could want, there was never any devoted love for either one. Later, I found that the marriage ended in a very bitter divorce heavily televised because of his status in life. The marriage ended with two children, a boy and a girl, Charles having custody of his son Jason whom he adored. Years later, when I met Jason, I learned that the feeling was mutual; he also was devoted son to his father and loved him very much.

What I do not understand is why was I being treated with such importance? Did everyone here know something that I did not? Since everyone seems to know so much about me, they also should know that I am not accustomed to such luxuries as private jets, hotel suites, and limousine rides. Not that I could not become accustomed to the total treatment.

I glanced across the room to see if I could sum up which one of these faces belonged to Mr. Jacobs. No one in the room seemed to fit the voice on the phone; I just knew that Mr. Jacobs would enter the room soon and put me out of my agony with an explanation of why my presence was required. Maybe he was going to open a call center and wanted me to run it. That would be exciting. Maybe the elderly gentlemen seated behind the solid oak desk, with what appeared to be leather bond file of all sorts, was Mr. Jacobs.

Those thoughts soon faded when the gentlemen behind the same desk rose and introduced himself as Bernard Willingham, Mr. Jacobs's attorney. Bernard laid several leather folders and legal tablets on his desk next to the ones that were already desk top and reached for his reading glasses out of a richly designed top desk drawer. Bernard examined the room to see if everyone was in attendance then asked for everyone's attention. Bernard started as he reseated himself. "For those present and who are not aware of the details of this meeting, Mr. Jacobs has passed away due to a tragic accident while traveling abroad." The news was very sad to hear, but what did that have to do with me? Bernard continued. "Due to stock and various other reasons, Mr. Jacobs's death has been kept of the uttermost secret. Only a few members of the board and I have been made aware of the details. Later this evening, a press release will be held. The seven gathered here today are called together for the reading of the last will and testament of James R. Jacobs III."

My mouth literally hit the floor with disbelief. I'm really confused as to why I am here. Reading of the will? I came to find that my dear customer was one of the world's richest men. He owned more companies than Van De Camps had pork and beans, and I'm at the reading of his will. Why?

Charles and Barbara seemed to be the only ones that were not anxiously awaiting the results, and were in total disbelief that we were all gathered together. I wondered why I was called all the way here to be left a postage stamp. What could this man possibly be leaving me? Bernard was the attorney of record and held power of attorney for Mr. Jacobs's affairs. I was surprised it was not Charles, but I guess Mr. Jacobs had need of several different attorneys for several different matters.

When Bernard saw that he had everyone's attention, again he began with matters that made me feel as if I had been living in the dark ages, and all the numbers and details went right over my head. Bernard read with patience, careful not to omit any details. Everyone present but me was left various dividends. Charles and Barbara had been provided with allotment to last the rest of their lives.

"Last but not least, I leave my remaining holdings and personal assets to Linda Morehouse, whom I've never met but had the pleasure of meeting in person only making her acquaintance over the phone. Although for a short time that only lasted nine minutes or so, Ms. Morehouse showed sincere concern for me and left a greater impact than anyone gathered in this room today outside of my assistant and attorneys." Bernard finished the reading of the will.

"The total amount from personal and company assets . . . To Linda Morehouse I leave"—the sound of a drum roll was beating in my ears. The first numbers I really heard was only "seventy-five," so I thought the next word would be dollars. The words I heard after that, I do not even know how to write on paper. The rest of the seventy-five was not dollars but went something like billion nine hundred thirty-two million eight hundred seventy-two thousand six hundred ten dollars and eight cents!" $75,932,872,610.08. I sat unmoving and thought that I had an audio problem. Did he say my name after that string of zeros, or was my name coming next? I thought I heard "to Linda Morehouse I leave seventy-five billion nine hundred thirty-two million eight hundred seventy-two thousand six hundred ten dollars and eight cents!. Not only was this man not from this planet, he owned it. I just could not connect my name to the amount of money I just heard. The eight cents, yes, I could relate to, but the rest of that information may as well been in a foreign language. When the numeric value of what I was now worth was revealed and realized, I thought I was going to die, not so much due to the amount but from the looks others gathered in the room sent my way, with the exception of Barbara and Charles. First thing I had to do was change my name to Jane Doe. Right after that thought, I fainted.

Barbara was the first person I remembered seeing after being revived a short while later. I was trying hard to remember who all these people were standing over me. Who is this woman fanning me, bent over with a glass of water in her hand? Did I get someone's pizza order incorrect? It only took a few more seconds of that delirium to remember why I fainted seventy-five billion nine hundred thirty-two million eight hundred seventy-two thousand six hundred ten dollars and eight cents worth of fainting! I should have been out for the count for the rest of my life. Nah, then I would not have been able to spend a dime. The concept of living with all that money did appeal to me, and I could learn to live with it. I wondered what I should change my name to.

Barbara, Charles, and Bernard all gave me their business cards in case I had need of contacting them. Had a need of contacting them? I said to myself, I need them now to count all this money . . . how many zeros am I worth, and can I now start shopping at Macy's?

I retained Charles and Barbara's services immediately. Contact them I did. The very next morning, I called Charles with so many questions he had to place me on hold to get a legal tablet. Mr. Jacobs was Charles's only client. I was going to need his assistance since he did such a great job with Mr. Jacobs as his attorney and financial advisor.

Charles and I agreed he would continue as if he were assisting Mr. Jacobs. I offered to write up a contract and was willing to pay him what Mr. Jacobs had been paying him to be at my disposal, but he declined. He agreed to assist with me setting up various bank accounts, strongly suggested stock options, and referred an accountant team that their firm used. After all that, if I found that I still needed his services, we would talk about retainer fees later. There were some small details of signing papers and disclaimers that I had to tend to which only took a couple of days. Thereafter, I was free to carry out my new life.

I phoned Charles and Barbara from time to time to attend to some money management needs that I now had. I did not need a management team before; who needed help with managing a four-hundred-dollar bank account? Barbara ended up being a close personal friend and advisor as well. I never knew large sums of money would require so much managing, but manage it they did.

I had a large sum put in trust with various holdings in companies that Charles and Barbara suggested, mostly the ones that Mr. Jacobs had owned or held large stock options in. I reinvested monies back in that had been liquidated at the time of Mr. Jacobs's demise. I had Charles and Barbara set me up a personal account with one million. I believe I can shop at Macy's with a million dollars and still have enough left for dinner out on the town.

Time to Change My Name

CHANGED MY NAME I did to Linda Nalley. It had a certain ring to it, and I thought it fit my new lifestyle perfectly. No Linda Nalley listed in the white pages either. Barbara helped with that undertaking and made sure all legal documents were in order consulting with Charles that my new legal name became Linda L. Nalley.

For the life of me, I do not know what I would have done without the two of them. Mr. Jacobs trusted them with all of his affairs—I guess I will do the same. This has been the craziest three weeks of my life. I've had to change all my phone numbers and find of course another place to reside. I flew back to California and took another two week vacation in case I was dreaming or someone detested the will, I would have a place of employment to return to. I went to my one-bedroom apartment to pack some important papers. All my remaining things, I called the Salvation Army to pick up. I registered in a nearby hotel under my new identification and went shopping at Macy's.

Barbara was a wiz and saw to it that my new identification came in a timely manager. Newspapers, groceries rages, and producers of talk shows, everybody was attempting to contact me for interviews. Somehow they were still able to locate me in my hometown even under my new name. Why do overnight success stories or loads of money have that effect on people? No one wanted to talk to me when I was serving pizza. Am I not the same person? I guess my life story was not exciting enough before. I can see it now walking home from work with reporters outside of my door: "Ms. Morehouse, Ms. Morehouse, how many pizzas did you serve today, and did you stand for five hours or six? Ms. Morehouse, wait, don't close the door; I have another question!" Where are all these people coming from now? Money, I tell you. Am I not the same person that flew to New York broke? But now I have worldwide coverage. What is that? I thought.

I am unsure if this capital gain was a curse or blessing. Long misplaced family from fourth cousins once removed attempted to contact me. In-laws by marriage, marriages twenty times removed. It was so comical and not comical at the same time. The rich and famous, I do not know how they did it. How does one discern true from false, needing help from being greedy? Anyone in my position would love to help within one's limit or reasoning. Some people seem to think anything one has in excess should be theirs for the asking, with the expectation of receiving. I just don't get it!

Once the story blew over on my overnight success, it settled down for a while. I tried everything I could to avoid the press for the simple fact that I wanted to be able to shop, drive, and perform daily activities without being mobbed. I kept a very low profile. I started to go to a country where no one spoke the English language; at least if I got mobbed with questions, it would not be in a language that I understood. I ruled out that thought and moved to Hawaii. A small villa suited my needs at the time while I wrapped up a few of life's baggage.

Next on my agenda was to pay some of my owed debts, money owed on bills and to friends and family members that had assisted me when the wind did not always blow favorable in my direction. I purchased my mom a home in Central California near other members of the family that she could visit with while I traveled in search of myself. Her home had a live-in nurse, companion, and housekeeper all wrapped in one. Her small estate came with a small pond. She loves to fish, so fish she shall. There would be a pond on the property stocked with her favorite fish. Semienclosed so she could go fishing 365 days a year if she wanted to. The contractors went crazy when asked to have heat and air where she would never get too hot or cold whenever she fished around her lake. A very short distance from her lake was a covered storage that resembled a small 7-Eleven for her bait and tackle needs and any refreshments that she may need while fishing. A bank account was set up with a million dollars. At over eighty years of age, her needs were minimal. That amount assured me that all of her needs would be met. If not, I am only a phone call away, and she would always know how to reach me. Many did not.

Feeling lonesome one day, I didn't know how I could have that feeling with all I had to do and the money to do it with, but I was. I contacted a number of close friends that stuck by me through thick and thin. One of my closest friends was Ciania Long. Ciania and I met while I was working at the phone company, and she has stuck with me through broken relationships, family problems, and job promotions. Ciania was always very protective of me. One day, I thought she was going to kill this one guy immediately for breaking my heart. She had plots of poisoned dinners, car crashes, and anything she thought for this guy to meet his demise for breaking my heart. It took everything I had in me to convince her that no one can do anything to you that is not allowed by you. I could have ended it long before heartbreak became heartbreak, early in the relationship when it would have only been a little loss of time and not a loss of mind. There were days early in the breakup where I almost did lose my mind. Thank God she was there for me. Although she's very funny, she also had a very dark side that makes me thankful she is my friend and not my enemy.

Ciania and I were so glad to talk to each other. We chatted on the phone from time to time for hours, catching up on events that were going on at the phone company where she was still employed and on what I'd been up to. Before I knew it, I had invited her out to the island for a visit. I could not wait to see her; I missed her so very much. I got tired of trying to dodge the world of reporters, and shopping alone was pure agony.

Ciania arrived about a week later on a chartered flight to the island. I informed her there was no need to pack because we were going to shop till we dropped. When she arrived at the island, we stayed up all night eating all types of polonaise food. We spoke of "The Call"; we always referred to Mr. Jacobs's call in that manner. "Linda, I still cannot believe that some stranger left you all that money," Ciania said.

"Ciania, I have it and don't believe it," I said.

Sometimes in the middle of the night, I go to the phone just to call the twenty-four-hour banking line to make sure I did not dream the whole thing and then ask, "Could you please confirm my available balance?" Together we laughed so hard we could not control our crying.

Ciania and I had breakfast first and then traveled all over the Hawaiian Islands. The weather was made to order for two longtime friends to spend the day together. Ciania was a good companion and friend that made me laugh all the time. Ciania has always had my best interest at heart, and I felt she would lay her life on the line for me if she had to. I was so glad she had the time to come spend it with me; it meant a lot.

Ciania remained a whole month on the island with me before going back to the States. We became closer than ever. We acquired new luggage to carry her wardrobe of new things back home with her, it was my pleasure to show her the time of her life.

With loads of pictures we'd taken from one side of the island to the next, she had an abundance of new memories. We both hugged and cried again, this time for a different reason. She and I had discussed the upcoming party I was to throw in a few months. With the promise from her to return for the party, I did not feel so sad to see her depart, but my heart still broke to see my friend go even for a short moment in time.

Four months after Ciania's departure, I gave a party in honor of friends and family. I called Ciania two weeks sooner than the scheduled party. We talked every day on the phone after she returned home, and she had been well briefed on all the details of the party, and even suggested a few ideas. she was so excited and could not wait to return to the island. She shared often how she wanted to pack up everything and move to the island forever. I asked Ciania if she would mind coming out a week earlier than the guest to be like a personal assistant and that I would hire her to help. "Of course," Ciania said, "but you do not have to pay me" she replied, but I insisted.

With the details of Ciania's arrival all arranged, I felt at ease. I spared no expense for the party, all the stops were pulled for first-class travel and lodging. My guest list included those who I care about and deserved all the attention that was relished upon them.

Guests started to arrive one day ahead of schedule. Thank God, my home was large enough to accommodate them. The party was a huge success for all intents and purposes. Checks were handed out anywhere from five thousand to twenty thousand dollars in gold trimmed envelopes, thanking everyone for his or her love and support until the day arrived that I could now love and show my appreciation for all that they have done for me.

Charles, Barbara, and Bernard were in attendance as well. They continued to be of assistance to me just like they were for Mr. Jacobs. Everyone appeared to be having a wonderful time but me. Looking around at the merriment of everything, I wondered out to the balcony alone . . . here it comes again . . . the eerie feeling that my mind and body are still not on the same accord, damn! What now? I was having the time of my life, and yet there was a void that I could not put my finger on. One would think that with all my financial needs met, I would rest easy.

Nonetheless, the feeling remained in my heart that I had back in my pizza serving days that I was destined for great things, and not great amounts of money. To somehow make a difference. Leave my mark in life and not a mark on life. At this time and place, I've yet to find my mark that I was to leave in life. I donated to churches and charities and still could not fill the void. What is this thing I am supposed to do? Life went on . . .

Shopping all over the world and now with sufficient wealth, I overlooked establishments like Macy's where I have desired to shop all my life. Funny how when one's finances change; their taste in things change as well. I shopped at stores that I could not even pronounce and bought clothes the same. It was designer shoes, clothes, and jewelry; if I could not locate it, I had it custom-made for me. I went to the finest salons for my hair and nails. I made appointment for facials and body rubs, a must for my new status in life. Went to Tiffany's and bought some moderate jewelry—one single-cut five-carat diamond ring for my right hand and a sleek-designed Rolex specially made thinner than most of their designs due to my small wrist. Last was a simple necklace with matching bracelet of quaint design. With my attire matching my bank account, still there was a void, even with the new look, I could not stop this feeling of uneasiness and misplacement for self-worth that has nothing to do with my new zeros in my bank account.

While I was searching around to find a permanent place to be in this world, the villa I was now in was rented. Becoming accustomed to living in Hawaii, I didn't have to look far. The climate was wonderful; this will be home. Going back to the cow town was not an option. Buying the villa I once rented I begun to fill it with things more to my taste. In its rented state, it was most lovely. However, now was the time to give it my personal touch. My two-week vacation ended so fast that I'd forgotten I was on vacation from a job at all, and it turned into a year. I felt secure enough that I did not report back to work. I'm sure at this point they had long since awaited my arrival back to work. I had no idea at the time that I would later own that same company and many more like it.

An Epiphany

ONE NIGHT, WHILE lying awake unable to sleep as I am unable to do most nights. (One would think that lying on six-hundred-count handwoven sheets, I would be able to sleep through a hurricane.) I had an epiphany! I would open the world's largest customer care center and dedicate it to Mr. Jacobs. This was to be a tribute to what a customer should be to customer service and not necessarily what customer service should be to a customer; it should be equally yoked. Just how am I to go about that task? I thought for a minute, this will not be like going to a fast-food chain. I will take one company, with water, gas, and telecommunications; hold the rudeness and I will have that to go! I sat straight up in my oversized bed, and reached for the phone to call Charles. With a sleepy-voiced hello, he said, "Linda it is four o'clock in the morning."

"Wake up, Charles!" I said, "You can do that when you're his only client."

"Charles, wake up," I said, "I want to buy something." Charles replied, "What in the world is it that you do not already have, Linda?" "Funny you would ask that question, Charles, what in the world, because that is it, Charles."

"What, Linda." Charles said, "you want to buy the world?"

"No, I don't want to buy the world, I want to own the world's largest call center.

"Why? Don't you have adequate phones or enough people to respond to your calls?" he said,

"Do not be coy, Charles," I said.

"Who would be calling you that it would require a call center to handle that type of volume?" Charles inquired.

"Everyone, I want to own the gas, water, and the electric company and all the holdings in the communications field."

"Linda, are you talking in your sleep?"

"No, I am not sleep talking, nor am I talking in my sleep," I replied. "I have been up all hours of darkness with this on my mind. It's going to cause total pandemonium, but I can handle it. I used to serve pizza, remember. I have sufficient resources to fund such a project, and, Charles, you are the greatest attorney in the world. Can we schedule at meeting here at the villa for breakfast a 6:00 a.m.?"

"Linda, did you forget I live in New York!" Charles said.

"For a split second, yes, I did. Tomorrow morning will be fine; same time, Charles, thank you," as she hung up.

I rose from bed at about 4:30 the very next morning. I could no longer sleep, nor did I desire to. I was too excited wondering how I was going to convince Charles that this was the right thing to do. I showered and dressed up in preparation for the meeting that was to take place shortly. Something comfortable and semiprofessional, I thought. What to wear for a 6:00 a.m. home power meeting? Nike from head to toe—the red jogging suit with white stripes will do. I selected a white spandex top, red-and-white matching running shoes, and neutral lipstick. Now I am ready for our meeting.

Charles arrived on time. I heard a soft chime of the doorbell, then the opening of the door.

"Linda, I'm here."

"Yes, Charles, I am in the kitchen." Charles entered the kitchen filled with the aroma of international coffee. Trying to focus on reading the *Wall Street Journal*, I glanced up over my reading glasses and said, "Good morning, Charles, thank you for being on time." Charles walked toward the kitchen counter and offered himself a cup of coffee. Pulling up a chair, he glanced over with a smile and simply said, "You're welcome, Linda, not a problem."

He wore a tan leisure suit, no tie around his light brown shirt tucked in under a Kenneth Cole brown leather belt. His feet were decked out with Italian light brown loafers. One look at him and I knew I should have chosen the Ann Kline sweat suit. I did not expect him to look any other way. Mr. GQ, I referred to him often, and he would just smile. What was this man doing in the law industry? He could make millions of dollars by simply smiling and standing there! Speech impaired. Charles was so handsome, but I just knew that I was not his type. In the back of my mind, I felt he thought I came from a world and background that differed from his. Even with my newfound fame and fortune, I felt as though I did not reach his standards to court.

"Linda, are you fully awake now?" Charles said. "Yes, I was fully awake last time we spoke I should say."

"I guess my question to you then, Linda, is, have you taken into account the full ramification of what this would entail even if we could get something like this off the ground?"

"Do you know what you are taking about here, Linda, a monopoly?"

"It will never happen!"

"Then, Charles, make it happen. Charles, nothing in life just happens until a sincere effort is put toward that something. Nothing has ever been achieved by osmosis or lack of effort. Charles, if it has happened please inform me how. Even with a winning lottery ticket you had to make an effort to buy one."

"What if we fail, Linda," Charles said.

"Then at least I could sleep at night knowing that we did our best. What I will not be able to do is sleep at night knowing that we did not turn over every stone in the universe with an attempt to do so! Charles, if everyone else waited on someone else to set the mark, the mark would never be set. I want to be the one to make the attempt to make and set the mark and standard, right here, right now."

"Charles, fear is premeditated failure, an opportunity presented unchallenged. A closed door will always remain a closed door until one makes an attempt to turn the doorknob. If at that time it is discovered the door is locked and you find yourself keyless, your attempt to leave was not a failure. The failure would be to assume a closed door is locked without turning that same doorknob. That's failure."

"Charles, I've yet to meet a successful person who did not try to be successful. There are more people unsuccessful who did not try then unsuccessful people who did! There are some people who look at the doorknob, Charles, and some who reach for the doorknob. Me, if the doorknob won't turn and I am keyless, I'd called the locksmith! But that's just me; I would not spend a lot of time pondering. If I can't open it, then I would call someone who could. If not us, then who; if not now, then when? The decision is made and the journey begins . . ."

"Linda, have you thought of a name for your vision?"

"Yes, Charles, of course. There is no other name could I give this dream but, Kusta'ma Kare."

Charles and I talked for hours concerning the how and whys of what this conversation meant. "Charles, I know this sounds like an unachievable goal, but I know that it can be done. This is not just for the money, Charles I have enough money and power. This is for Mr. Jacobs. With all his money and all his power, he was the kindest customer I had ever encountered. With all Mr. Jacobs stood for, he had time to say thank you and did not for one second take for granted that it was my job to help him. Unlike most, others feel like a paycheck should be thanks enough. He gave me hope, that there was still compassion for another in this world we live in today. Because of him, you and I sit and talk for hours. Yes, I want a monopoly to achieve a greater goal. New world order of a human kind, human awareness, if you must, Charles, is what I am talking about. We as people have forgotten simple kindness to say thank you, please, a simple good morning for Christ's sakes! I want to turn the tables where kindness is no longer an option but mandatory, until it becomes second nature. No one will know my real reasoning behind this venture but you and I, Charles. Mr. Jacobs would be proud. He must have felt the same way, at the reading of the will; it stated that only a handful of you in this room "ever made me feel the way Ms. Morehouse did in nine short minutes." What does that tell you, Charles? He knew what I knew about mankind; we tend to get so lost in ourselves that basic kindness is forgotten by most. Why do you think Mr. Jacobs and I appreciated each other so much? Nine minutes, nine minutes was all it took for the two of us, and some people spend all day together and do not say half the things Mr. Jacobs and I said to one other in nine little minutes. Whenever I was having a bad day at work, I would think of Mr. Jacobs to make me smile. Charles, you have to make this happen."

"Yes, Linda, I agree for Mr. Jacobs," he said. I responded for mankind.

"Charles, if people would just think about that word for a minute, 'mankind,' not 'man mean.' Think about it where did mankind go? The operative word here, Charles, is *kind*, and Mr. Jacobs was a kind man."

For weeks, it seemed that all Charles did was make phone calls and attend meetings. I believe that Charles, Barbara, and Bernard were busier than they had ever been for Mr. Jacobs. Conference calls were endless, fax and e-mails ever coming. Charles called almost screaming, "Linda, we are going to need some more help." Help they got. When wind of what was transpiring got out, people wanted to commit Charles to an asylum and me along with him. For the ones that saw the vision and the business opportunity, he got more unsolicited help than he could ever use. Day in and day out, phones ringing, fax going, it was a whirlwind of activities. I could feel the excitement of what was to come and the dread of what I would have to endure as a result of this major decision. Before it was all over, I'd wish I had bought a singing group instead to entertain me, but the wheels are in motion; there will be no turning back.

Well it took three years to put everything together. A lot of litigations etc . . . . What came next was enough to make me change my mind, but I prevailed. Filing business licenses was the small task. Before all effective companies can finalize the deal, Kusta'ma Kare must also gain approval from the five-member Federal Communications Commission (FCC). The commission is believed to be in the final stage of its review. By contrast, the role of the FCC is to approve the transfer of spectrum licenses and consider the deal's impact on "the public's interest." The Department of Justice was also present, but it served a different purpose also; it had to consider the impact of a singly own company of this magnitude would have. Didn't hurt that I had enough money to pay off the U.S. national debt we owed to Japan, and I did make a very large contribution.

With negotiations up and running, I was busier than ever. More often than not, I barely noticed that the eerie feeling was crawling in the other direction down my back, instead of up my back as it has done for so many years. I did however feel my mind was clear as a bell, meaning that at times we filled the same space from time to time. What can I say; at least it's making more cameo appearances, which is more than it's been doing over the last few years of my life.

The Call Centers

NEWS FLASH, CNN ... *Wall Street Journal* ... Today the U.S. Department of Justice announced its stamp of approval for the largest singly owned multibillion dollar company Kusta'ma Kare.

After the buy outs, the national debt I paid to Japan, and other companies acquired, I only had a few million dollars left, and revenue from Kusta'ma Kare would pull me out of the red soon.

With millions out of work, due to this massive takeover, I knew I would have to do something, or the economy would plummet and unemployment would be at an all-time high. So I employed the best of the best employees from every company that I bought. I recruited a team to review all company employees' files. I hired all employees with good work records from all companies that were also paid at Kusta'ma Kare wages. Kusta'ma Kare employees were filtered out through a number of departments such as billing specialist, service engineers, technical service, and maintenance engineers, and of course, customer service representatives.

Since Kusta'ma Kare was the water, gas, and communication company, there was plenty of work to save at least 71 percent of the work forces that would have otherwise ended up in the unemployment line. Billing was one of my largest departments. The current base of over one hundred million customers all wanting something for nothing would soon find they could no longer have what they want. Customer service representatives disconnecting calls and talking down to customers are no longer allowed.

Ten fifteen-story buildings strategically placed throughout the United States awaited the launch simultaneously. I started to make Kusta'ma Kare locations in major cities but decided against it because of too many threats. The media coverage of the launch has covered both positive and negatives reviews, more on the latter. I survey small towns no more than one hour away from major cities convenient for commuting. The call centers were numbered one to ten; call center one in Northern California found a great location in Eureka, California, outside of Redding, which I made my stateside corporate office. I had my work cut out for me, not labor wise, but decision-making was tiring. Floor plans had to be designed differently for different states due to weather conditions. Call center two was located in Lompoc, Southern California, outside Bakersfield. Call center three was in Steamboat Springs, Colorado. Call center four was in Montana, in the town of Billings. Texas was so large I put two locations. Call Center five was in Amarillo, and number six in Brownsville. Number seven was located in Swainsboro, Georgia; number eight in Bangor, Maine. With only two more locations to go, I built in Fort Dodge, Iowa, held building number nine. Last location for Kusta'ma Kare ten we built in Parkersburg, West Virginia.

I traveled so much that company jets were a must (we had four); it also helped in security measures as well. Sometimes, my movements were so restricted I thought I was a national treasure. All locations were chosen with a land clear of three square miles, a small landing strip, enclosed parking lots two levels high with entrances direct to the call centers, and temperature control. Landscaping varied, depending on the locations, from palm trees to cacti. All the locations had outdoor cafés that I named Jacob's Café with specialty coffees, ice creams, yogurts, and smoothies. Patio and lounges were available for lunches and breaks if one chose not to eat at our indoor restaurants. There was one convenient store at each location, for the small needs one may have during the course of a workweek. Beautiful, I must say to myself.

I took special care to design all the Kusta'ma Kare call centers with my employees in mind. With all the stress, I knew they would have to tolerate the first year or so with irate customers. I wanted them to have every comfort a professional environment has to offer. Walking around admiring how things were coming along made me want to work again in the customer care field and sing my jingle! (♫ I was born to be a customer service rep! ♫). Had this been the case when I was employed in the customer field, maybe I would not have been so inspired to open call centers. On second thought, yes, I would have; the world needed all the help it could get. People were out of control with rudeness and self-importance.

One thing that I will not lose touch with is how I felt big businesses should treat their employees. Never forget to take care of the people who take care of your business. You don't make billions and pay pennies, and you will surely get your money's worth. Hire the best-qualified employees for the position and pay them qualified salaries. I don't care if it is flipping burgers. If your company commercials are viewing five hundred times a day in different languages, why are people paid pennies to serve them? I don't understand. You have laborers who are building million-dollars home who cannot afford to even buy one let alone one at that cost. I don't understand. I do understand that my concept of employee treatment will far superexceed any other in employment history bar none. I do not want to be driven in a limousine to my office while my employees are forced to take public transportation, and since I am in the position to dictate policy, there it is. Happy employees generate happy customers; happy customers generate revenue, triple-win situation.

There would be no chain of command; every one was trained a manager at all levels of their departments, only two supervisors per department head. There was no complaint department, only four functions: new service, payment, billing, and technical support. Dress code strictly professional; no jeans, tee shirts etc . . . .

I invested in top-of-the-line equipment, lunchroom with professional chefs, and restroom attendants. Salary was straight across the board no matter what state you were located, ten thousand a month. No union or medical benefits provided and discussed during interviews, and contracts were signed at hire. Providing these salary employees could afford good health care. No union is needed because there were no negotiations; you report to work or you were fired. Kusta'ma Kare provided five-days-per-year sick leave with pay, all recognized national holidays off. Kusta'ma Kare had enough employees where we could rotate work schedules nine months and three months off, if applied for, and approved at the beginning of the years which voided out sick leave with pay time off and national holidays. Business hours of operation were eight to five, Monday through Friday, closed for lunch from twelve to one thirty. Kusta'ma Kare was open to employees from 7:00 a.m. to 7:00 p.m. for breakfast or dinner after or before business hours. All Kusta'ma Kare locations had private gyms and day care on site. Employees who came over from the buyout after one year of employment would max out at ten thousand a month. Payroll had two floors with over twelve thousand employees for all three companies, also located at the Eureka office; they were in charge of payroll for Kusta'ma Kare, Jacobs Trust, and Jacobs Security. Jacobs Trust was a financial institute just for the three firms and employees of either firm; Jacobs Security guarded only the three companies and did not contract out to any other company.

Interviews and board meetings had to be held constantly. I hired the best of everything not just for Kusta'ma Kare, but for all the business that had to support Kusta'ma Kare. Top fight security of course was a must. I have already had more death threats than Saddam Hussein and the president combined. I bought a security company and hired former military, secret service, and police officers. When you have a monopoly on the nation's pulse and lifeline, you begin to wonder why your dog is looking at you strangely today, and if he may have been kidnapped and turned into a trained assassin. Maybe I should get rid of the dog, get a caged bird . . . a fish . . . turtle, something harmless that cannot be trained and become a deadly assassin. I had to remember little Jacob was only a miniature terrier; I had earrings bigger than his teeth.

The team, as I referred to us, had four members: Bernard, Barbara, Charles, and I. The team now staffed with thirty including Barbara, Bernard, and Charles. We had accountants, bookkeepers, four public relations personnel, five more attorneys; litigations, criminal law, human rights, civil, and corporate law.

Our team stays in the air more than on land for signing of legal documents that could not be faxed and putting a lot of finishing touches from companies purchased and government contract for Kusta'ma Kare business. Charles was given power of attorney. He and I could not be in the same place at the same time. Barbara had power of attorney for Charles, and of course, Bernard had Barbara's. We had many meetings on and off the island. The launch date for Kusta'ma Kare has been set. Jacob Trust was up and running along with Jacob Security. One ribbon-cutting ceremony would suffice for all, and it will be held at the branch in Eureka, California.

My staff was trained and prepared for what was to come as a result this monopoly. Some would fade out due to the stress, but those that remained would enjoy all the benefits that Kusta'ma Kare had to bestow upon their employees.

All company employees were paid the same whether you were security, bank teller, or customer care calls, repairs, technical service, or mopping the floors. If you fell under the Kusta'ma Kare umbrella that owned the other companies, you were paid the same. Simple, thinking I thought now I do not have to get worried about bankers trying to be customer service, customer service trying to be security. Everyone's job was important to me and deserved the same pay. Kusta'ma Kare and all employees under the umbrella of companies were paid the same—ten thousand a month.

When I was not at the office, or flying the friendly skies, I found the villa most comforting. A two hundred acre island off the shores of the Hanamaulu Island in Hawaii held my new home. A private landscaping company that specialized in commercial properties flew in, and it took about a year to have it totally redone to my specifications. I needed a clearing of about fifteen acres to house the villa and corporate office. The villa stood only two stories on completion; the villa and office totaled ten thousand square feet (eight for the house and two for the office). I could venture between my home and office without ever stepping outdoors in the event of bad weather. My corporate office on the island is where all legal documents and other holdings and personal and corporate information were held; the headquarters for Jacobs trust and Jacobs Security could be monitored and managed from the island as well.

With the island totally secured and only accessible by air, or sea, I felt safe. Although Hawaii has beautiful weather, it can turn strange. Hurricane awareness I could not overlook. I had a nine-hundred-square-foot storm cellar fully equipped with a generator and enough supplies to last a month. It had computers, satellite phones, and radio bands for weather reports. I think my real reason was that if anyone ever flew over and bombed my island, I would have somewhere to go until help arrived. There were floor doors that led to my cellar/bomb shelter from my home and office.

My bedroom was a masterpiece of loveliness. Pedestal bed fit for a queen. Trimmed in gold and ivory, a hint of palm tree green throughout the room blended with the island's surrounding landscape. The entire villa was accented the same. There were three swimming pools, with flowing waterfalls, although I had to learn to swim first. But it did not discourage me from designing them nonetheless. Pools first, learn to swim second. I say having the pools would give me the motivation to learn. The finished result was a place that I thought I would never visit or own in this lifetime or the next. I would guess now the only reason I have sleepless nights is I felt at times if I slept too long, I would wake up and find it was all a dream.

I had another small bungalow with three bedrooms and a generous office built. Charles frequented the island too often for business, and I felt that he should have his own privacy verses having to stay at the villa. Charles had one of the bedrooms designed for Jason, with computers and high-tech stereo systems. Jason studied more than he did anything else and enjoyed classical music. Charles came to the island about 40 percent of the year during the good weather season; and when he was not here, he was at his penthouse in the States.

I trusted Charles with my life. So I had no problem trusting him with my company or money. There was something about him when he looked at me. He seemed very devoted to me on a different level than most. I know he was not money driven; he was rich and powerful in his own right. Maybe it was the challenge of Kusta'ma Kare, and with Mr. Jacobs gone, I guess that he had nothing to do with his days. On days when it was unbearable I thought surely he would walk, but he'd just smile with a reply, "I will handle it, Linda, things will be fine." Charles never went on dates to my knowledge, nor did I, who had the time. When it was convenient, he saw his son Jason that I finally had the opportunity to meet. Jason was a young handsome man a younger version of his dad, and I enjoyed his company when he did come to visit his dad.

Launch date for all ten of the call centers was set for two months. Training for employees was six months since everyone had to be trained in all facets of the company for their departments. The goal is not to be mean and heartless, but firm and nonbending is the new game in town. There is something about having only one choice for services rendered that will make you humble. If there were only one man to woman ratio for life, you would have a tendency to either treat that mate with love and respect or spend the rest of your life by yourself. Threatening to take your business down the street if we don't give you what we want and finding that we are the only business in town, you will have a tendency to pay your bills on time, and levels of disrespect tend to lessen.

Choices are all about free will. When your choice is dictated by another's action, it is no longer free will. It becomes a reaction from an action driven by another. At the same time, our customer service representative will no longer be short-tempered with heavy sighs rushing through your concerns. You cannot cure one problem without curing the other. Customer abuse by customer service representatives would not be tolerated by me at all; those are grounds for immediate termination without discussion. The first few years are going to be hard enough. My training team taught patience first, understanding second, and nontolerance last for anyone giving less to him or her. Bad language from customers gives us the right to inform the customer that if they continue on this path of communication, we have the right to disconnect the call. The customer can call back when they have calmed down, and that information must still be delivered with respect.

We were in the final week before opening day. I visited all ten locations to assure everything was up to standards and that all employees were comfortable. I checked on all the restaurants, chefs in white hats, and aprons with smiles. Kitchens were all sparkling clean. The cafés were stocked and ready to go. The grounds were manicured and spotless. Everything well superexceeded my expectations, and I was very satisfied. Faces were glowing. I felt that all the call centers show be placed in *Omni* magazines; they had topnotch technology. I walked through and introduced myself to as many employees as possible. It appeared everyone was eager and ready to launch.

My board of director was brought on as advisors. A contract was written up that on retirement a percentage of the company would be provided; they included family and close friends that I trusted with my life. I first brought in Barbara, whom I could not live without. I love her most because she was a tiger, a go-getter and never tiring force, and my lifeline. Thanks, Barbara, for not being at work the day the heavens opened when your boss called and changed my whole life. Next, we have Karen, seven years now my friend. She has been with me since my pizza-serving days, broken relationships, and business ventures. I had to bring her on board.

Karen is single also. Why are all the people in my life single? I have to admit that I do not like a lot of gatherings with married couples. Karen is loyal as the day is long. She has a very sweet spirit and is a hard worker and a faithful friend. I still can't fathom why she has not married; all her children are grown and self-sufficient. But I guess that will be her story to tell, not mine to tell for her. The last friend I brought aboard is very important; her love for me, right or wrong, is very strong. Yes, Ciania Long came to work for me. I have to tell you a little more about Ciania Long, or CL she is as better known.

Ciania has keen senses and is sensually beautiful and dangerous. She is my constant companion, driver, and head of security. Ciania's hair is long, sleek, and black. She wears all black. Soft-spoken and always underestimated, but she clings to my side like heat to the sun. It was my good fortune to have her for a friend, and the CIA's lost not to recruit.

Ciania hired herself when we spoke on the phone after her visit to Hawaii. When she heard that I was opening a call center and everything, she was reading in the news. Her response to me was "who is going to look after you?" Her next words to me were "I am on my way." I hired her right off as an extension of myself, her position undefined as of yet, until the day we started interviewing for my personal bodyguards. She and Charles sat in on those interviews. I think they should marry each other; they are so much alike. During the interview process for my bodyguard, she felt no one filled the qualifications for my safety. I don't know why I am surprised after hundreds of applicants and twenty-six interviews there was none of course that Charles or Ciania would approve. Ciania finally hired herself. Charles approved. Surprised, I am not.

Ciania, although my friend and now the protector of my life, is a handful; she bulletproofed all my cars and tinted the windows so dark that not only could no one see in, I had to ask her the weather condition due to the fact I could not see out the windows. Ciania goes a little over the top, but her efforts are worth it. I sleep a lot better at night knowing she is in charge of my safety. Sometimes, I think she never sleeps since she has taken on my welfare; it has become her mission in life. If I was a superhero and depended on my cape to support me in flight, my cape's name would be Ciania Long. Everyone in life should have a friend just like her.

My family members consisted of one brother and three sisters. My bother John is the oldest of the five and wise as his years. My oldest sister Jude, our family leader, agreed to come aboard. The last three of us, Carrie, Marilyn, and I, take turns being leaders depending on who is present. I am the last one born and the last to succeed. All salaries were enough for everyone that I hired, and they walked away from any current income one hundred percent satisfied. I would have it no other way, and to keep down competition, everyone was hired the same. I believe board members are elected since Kusta'ma Kare started from scratch, there was no shareholders and no one to vote in, so I hired!

Well, there you have it, our team and members of the board: Linda, Barbara, Bernard, Charles, Ciania, John, Jude, Carrie, Marilyn, and Karen of Kusta'ma Kare. Ten members of the board ready and fully aware of the battles that lie ahead of us. Were we really ready for the journey?

Chaos

MY PRIVATE OFFICE in the states was located in Eureka, California, atop of call center number one. A larger version of the Hawaii office, this office location was eighteen hundred square feet of lamb-woven, high-pile, natural-tone carpets. My desk was white marble with gold trimmings and topped with glass, deep rich white lounge sofa, and chairs. There was a small sitting area with a wet bar that I stocked with sparking fruit-flavor water, juice, and soda. No alcohol is allowed in any of the corporate offices or on the grounds. I felt if you needed to drink at work, you should not be at work. I chose not to drink, not that I'm opposed to people that did; I just do not promote it in the work environment or business meetings—it clouds one's insight to make a business decision. Why is it that so many business meetings are held over cocktails? I thought I would not delegate my business dealing to anyone making a decision with a scotch on the rocks in one hand and a contract in the other. Why do you think it's called a cock's tail when you can't see right side up; if it were so productive, it would be called something like a brain stimulator instead of a cock's tail. "Hey, everyone, after work let's go for a mind enhancer. My treat!" Few would show up and the libraries would be full at happy hour and the bars empty.

Adjacent to my office of course was Ciania's office similar to mine but was in black and gold with a two-way mirror so she could see the comings and goings to my office. She also had a hidden gun rack and an arsenal that should have belonged to the United States Army. We have got to get her some help. I did not know that when we worked at the call center, in her pastime, she was at the gun range, and her favorite movie was *A Time to Kill*

Charles had an office right across the hall from mine. There were only five that had access to the private elevator that lead to the penthouse offices. With Charles only across the hall, Ciania to my left, Barbara and Bernard to my right, I never had to venture far to chat in person with the four people that held my heartstrings.

Well the day has come for the grand opening of Kusta'ma Kare. After visiting all the call centers, I was finally back in my California office. The ribbon-cutting ceremonies for all the companies turned out a big success.

On day one, I sat at my desk awaiting the first calls from one of the call centers with a number of issues that could arise. All was quiet for the first few days. The concept of combining water, gas, and electricity with communications all on one bill was really not that hard to do. The bills were easy to read, itemized, and came up with a combined balance. Most customers appreciated that fact that only one check had to be written each month for some many amenities. I came to find later as years went by that customers preferred to pay their bills a year in advance with us due to the fact that there was no negotiating. We said a sweet, kind, but firm "No, unfortunately, I am unable to assist with that request! In what form would you like to make that payment?" This was the case the first few months in many homes and companies not wanting to pay thinking this company's life span was short-lived and that they would move to a hotel in the meantime or find rooms for rent. Little did they know we were here to stay.

Many conversations in homes I am sure went a little something like this,

"Henry, the lights are off again. Did you call Kusta'ma Kare?"

"No, Susan, when I tried to call, the phone was off too! Why didn't you call last week, Susan?"

"Henry, you know I was not going to call Kusta'ma Kare and tell them we did not have the money until the end of the month!" Some nice person with a smiley voice would have said, "What date would you be able to make payment? I understand service will be restored on that date. Thank you for calling Kusta'ma Kare."

"Susan, drive over to your mother's and ask to use her credit card, then use her phone to call Kusta'ma Kare, and get our services turned back on!"

"Henry, I will. But you have to promise to stop losing your temper when you call, they are very nice people, but you cannot curse at them when you don't have the payment, then it goes off before it's even due."

The only time we ran into trouble was when bills could not be paid that instead of losing one utility, they would collectively lose all. Agreements for large companies, state-government owned, had special rates, and taxes were minimal. Negotiations are never fun, but I did the best I could to be fair. To top guns with lawyers attempting to pressure us for better rates, I simply stated, "better rates than whom?" You should see my bills with ten call centers with modems, faxes, and more communication devices than I want to pay for, and I own the company! How can I expect others to pay their bills when I am unwilling to pay my own!

There were no contracts to sign, and any termination fees or signing fees—we had no need for them. There was absolutely no one else to sign with, so what was the point? Unless you lived in some small rural area that had independent companies, there were no choices. I had no desire to bid for the independent companies in those areas.

For the first year it was denial. Customers all over the U.S. from residential, small businesses, and some large corporations were outraged. How could this happen, how could one person, one company, be in control of their entire major necessities? We stayed calm, and handled the calls as they came, many threats of lawsuits for which I was prepared. Many were indeed filed, none won. The courts had to pay their bills too.

The second year, I had two bomb threats in two different states and had to clear the entire buildings for the day all over the states. The threat came By way of the security desk phone, five months apart, and after evacuation of all employees, both times no bombs were ever located in either occurrence. But to take precautions, I would all clear all ten call centers for the entire day, and since no one was able to take payments, no service was interrupted.

At times, I felt like throwing in the towel. Was it worth what I was putting my employees through? "Mr. Jacobs, what have

I done?" I said aloud. I have put hundreds of lives in danger for my selfish desires. Then a vortex of emotion went in and out of me like a draft. Then for the first time in my life, I had a crystal-clear thought—for a strong wall to be built, some bricks must be broken. As soon as the thought came, it left. Stranger than that is the courage that it left me with to continue. I had never felt mind and body closer than they are right now.

The media had a field day with the information of the bomb threat. "Kusta'ma Kare has closed down several of its operations today as news of bomb threats, employees flee, fearful for their lives." I was sure that the company would go under and that employees would file all types of lawsuits. The very next day, I had my manager of each building call me with reports of attendance activities, of how many employees showed up, if any. Reports from all ten call centers came in throughout the day, with the different time zones reporting the numbers in attendances. By the end of the day, all reported to work on time, and most were early. Not one employee filed a lawsuit, from my customer service representatives to the sanitation engineering staff. All were very supportive and understanding. Many sent letters of love and support. I had Barbara send out official letters of appreciation to each and every employee for all the centers for their support, and dedication. The slanderous news from the media eventually died down about one week after the dreadful day of the bomb threats.

On year three, things had seemed to settle down somewhat as opposed to the previous two years. Small lawsuits here and there, someone sitting in the dark—no doubt, bills unpaid. The media still carried a lot of controversies from interviews from other large company's heads that had gone under as a result of the massive takeover. Unconstitutional this and unconstitutional that; I even remember one day reading someone quoting that I had lost my mind and the Kusta'ma Kare wouldn't last a year. Well, we are well into year three and approaching year four. Not incident free, but holding on.

The *Wall Street Journal* was always very optimistic, and I have yet to read anything by the journalist assigned to writing about Kusta'ma Kare that has stopped my from buying my favorite paper. Thank goodness.

Missing

NOW GOING INTO year four, one winter day, I convinced Ciania to let me take a walk. She screamed to the high heavens no. "Ciania, calm down, I know that it is cold and raining outside, and I feel like a short walk to the deli I will cover up well."

"Linda," she said "you have eight chefs on the ground, why can't you order something up?"

"Ciania, you make me feel like a prisoner sometimes. I understand my safety is your primary concern, but so should be my peace of mind, or well-being should I say."

"Okay, Linda let me grab my gun."

"See, that is what I am talking about. I am not a prisoner going on the Big Yard for a walk among gang members; I am only going down the street for a sandwich."

"Okay, Linda, have it your way, but I expect you back within the hour, or I will come and look for you." I walked out of the office door toward the private elevator looking over my shoulder back at Ciania saying, "stop worrying so much!"

As I walked down the raining street of the Eureka's, sidewalks, it was a cold bitter day. I should have taken a cab or called for the limousine. I grabbed the lapels of my coat to chase away the harsh winds that slapped a crossed the back of my neck. I only had a few more blocks to go. My favorite sandwich with chowder is just what the weather ordered. My mouth watered, as it had been some time since I had visited this wonderful sub sandwich shop that made a great tuna on rye.

I guess the real reason I wanted to walk alone for the last few weeks was that I had been unable to sleep. There was a deep-pitted fear inside me. Not the eerie feeling though that I have grown accustomed to; this is different. The crowded streets were busy with people rushing to and fro, going God only knows (and them of course) where. I hope the sub shop is not very busy.

Standing at the crosswalk, I noticed a lurking car driving slower than most cars on the street for that time of day, and then it drove forward.

I waited to cross the street and for that little green running man that resides in the little black box to stop sleeping and permit me to do so. Finally, I can across the street. Now if I now run, that little green guy is in a hurry to go back to sleep and does not stay in the walk/run position very long.

Great, when I got to the sub shop, the line was out the door. Ciania's going to kill me; it is going to take all day at this rate. Finally, it took almost forty-five minutes to get my sandwich. Now I do not have the time to sit and eat it. I thanked the person that took my order and stated it is to go please!

Standing at the crosswalk again at the opposite side of the street of Kusta'ma Kare, I am again waiting on the green running man to show up to give me his approval to walk across the street. It began to rain. Thinking to myself while hunger pains stabbed away at my stomach, I may as well take a nibble of my sandwich; that little green guy in the black box sometimes takes very long naps.

Looking around, I noticed that it had gotten later than I thought. The hustle of people had ceased. The five o'clock rush had slowed to a crawl, and the streets were near empty. I held my head down; I know for only a second to open up my little white paper bag with one hand on, my umbrella in the other, trying desperately to Take a small nibble of tuna on rye. Then suddenly, everything went dark! Before anyone or I myself knew what happened, a limousine pulled up, and I thought it was the company limo and that Ciania had came to look for me. The back doors of the limo swung open, and before I could defend myself or make a sound, it all happened so fast that I never had a chance to see who had put something over my head. The last thing I remembered before it went dark was dropping my tuna and rye to the ground.

Four hours later, when I had not yet return to the office or called, Ciania thought to herself, something has happened. Ciania could not reach Charles or Barbara, but she continued to try. "What am I thinking, try calling Linda. Before you make another call and upset everyone, Linda could be on the elevator on her way up." Ten more minutes went by, no Linda, and Ciania only got a busy signal when attempting to reach my cell phone.

Ciania went through her arsenal for an array of handguns that she could carry concealed. Out the same office door and private elevator she went. "My God, Linda's missing." Panic filled every part of Ciania's body as she continued an attempt to reach the others: Charles, Barbara, and other members of the board. Ciania's last thought when the elevator door closed behind her was "I knew I should not have let her have her way. Charles is not going to understand this. Linda has not had the privilege of seeing Charles's mean streak I have when it comes to Linda and her safety," Ciania thought as she awaited the elevator.

Ciania remembered one day while taking the limousine through the car wash when Linda was in the back reading her favorite past time the *Wall Street Journal*,.

"Ciania, how long is this going to take? Are we getting a regular wash or the works?" Linda asked.

"Why, Linda? What do you have in mind now?" asked Ciania

Linda stepped out of the car before I could stop her for refreshment; it is almost like Charles had built-in radar when it came to Linda. The limo phone rang the same time the car door closed. "Ciania, I need to speak with Linda, would you transfer the line." The only thing I remembered after I said she stepped out for a minute was words I thought only Satan himself could say.

I'm on my way; the next thing I heard was click as the line went dead.

I wondered when Charles was going to realize that he was in love with Linda.

Ciania remembered looking at her watch when Linda closed the elevator door. It was two thirty; it is now way after six. Ciania took her personal car—a Corvette—to the sub shop. She thought it is much faster than attempting to walk.

Where the hell is everybody! Ciania tried not to panic when she was not back within an hour and now look what has happened. Ciania drove like the wind to the sub shop, and the sales clerk remember her ordering to go. Ciania rode up and down the Eureka streets looking for accidents. She saw none. Ciania went back to the office in case I had returned unnoticed by her. Ciania rushed through the lobby, advised security to check all badges face to badge, carefully entering and leaving, and has Ms. Nalley been seen entering the building? Yes, yes, no was all the guard could say to Ciania. Ciania rode the elevator back to the penthouse office to see if Linda had come in through her private entrance. Running through the door, Ciania cried out, "Linda, Linda!" only the echo of her own voice bounced off the walls.

When the phone did begin to ring, it did not stop. The first call was from Charles; I did not know an individual could ask so many questions without taking a breath. Charles's voice was like blows to Ciania's ears and heart. Ciania, what have you done? I do not care what Linda said. Once again Ciania heard, "I'm on my way," then the line went dead. The next call came from Barbara in tears, "Ciania, did I hear your message correctly, Linda is missing?"

The next morning, all members of the board congregated in the boardroom trying to discern just what could have happen. With a small degree of not really facing what could have happened. The one thing that no one wanted to do was to alert the authorities. The board took a vote. Unanimous to steer clear of media coverage of this at all cost.

Ciania was the first to stand in the room to give us a briefing of what Linda was wearing and opinion of Linda's mood. Did she just up and run off? She was very adamant about going alone? "No, Linda would not have done that," Charles stated. "Then where is she?" Barbara said next. The nine members of the board including her family agreed that Linda, although she's had a rough time in life she is a very levelheaded person. "If she did run off, she would have left a note so as not to worry us all stating she needed some time alone," Karen said.

"Linda could have gone home to Hawaii for that her sister Jude spoke up. There is something else afoot here," Jude concluded. Her brother John took the floor. "Just a minute, everyone, are we overlooking the obvious? I know that no one wants to say the 'K' word but let's get realistic. What we needed to decide at this moment is what we are going to do when the phone does ring and who was going to answer it. It had still been under twenty-four hours since anyone here has seen Linda. My prayer was that when the phone rang, they would ask for money and that on the six o'clock news her body had not been discovered. Someone could as easily want her dead in lieu of money; it depends on who has her. Kusta'ma Kare has created a lot of controversy as well as enemies. Let's just pray Linda is kidnapped and not dead. Kidnapped we can handle."

All the members of the board were secure in the event anything happened to either one of them. There were safes with millions of dollars all in the event something like this occurred. This way, the bank would not have to tie us up with a lot of red tape. Even Jacobs Trust would have to be opened and the bank president notified. What if the kidnappers wanted the money at 4 a.m. and called at 1 a.m.? One hundred million dollars was stored in five different locations throughout the state in the event we needed money in a hurry. None of the locations was more than two hours away from each other in a helicopter ride.

For the first time in four years, we saw Ciania cry. "Ciania, we do not blame you," Barbara said, "Linda could be extremely bullheaded at times.""I know," said Ciania, "but I should have followed her anyway."

I arose in a room that was very sinister, dark, and cold. I was barely waking and unable to tell what type of room I was in; it had no lighting at all for me to see exactly where I was. I looked around my immediate surroundings, down at the floor, at what type of bed I had arisen from. I could scarcely see from my swollen eyes. Shivering with dread and from the cold, I tried to commit to memory what exactly had happened.

That last thing I remembered was ordering tuna on rye in the deli down street from the office, standing at the crosswalk, and waiting on the little green man. Ciania's going to kill me, if whoever has me does not kill me first. She warned me not to go out alone, but I always have to have my way. Now look at what my way has gotten me into. Sometimes, others tell us things for our safety and not for our confinement; it was not Ciania's suggestion that confined me, but my failure to comply.

My stomach began to growl from lack of a tuna-on-rye sandwich. I could feel the cold air burning my skin through my tattered clothes. The cot that I laid upon had broken down springs that made me change positions when I sat in one place for too long. What else was one to do when confined in a dark, damp dungeonlike room? Think, Linda, what to do. I could not think. What am I saying, think? Your mind must be present to think. Still being a coward, my mind once again had an agenda all its own. Maybe my mind is out there somewhere trying to find an escape route, hopefully, looking for a way out for the both of us, and this time it wouldn't have to fight hard for me to follow.

I was still in a state of confusion as I glanced around my surroundings. The room where I sat had no windows and had a steel huge door. Of course, I'd check to see if it was locked. As I tried to stand, my legs wobbled; they must have roughed me up pretty well, but why can't I remember anything? I think my legs are wobbly due to hunger. I finally made my way to the still door. I found myself standing in front of a very large gray steel door with no doorknob, just a key hole.

Wow! We always have to remember what we quote to another about what they should do in life. I remember a conversation years ago in the kitchen with Charles about how failure is measured in the trying or the not trying. After that thought, with all the might I could muster, I pressed up against the gray steel door . . . waited as if the gates from heaven were going to swing open. The enormous gray door did not budge. I had to try.

Sliding to the floor, I began to cry, and cry, and cry some more. Linda, get a grip, you don't have enough energy to cry. God only knows when you're going to get some food if at all. No cell phone to call anyone, no one to hear my deepest darkest fears. I did not even want to process my deepest darkest fears at this time let alone share them with anyone else!

After what seemed to be an eternity but in actuality had only been two days, I was famished. No one has come to check on me or to bring me anything for nourishment. I had heard no noise from the other side of that large leviathan of a thing called a door. There was a plastic bucket in the corner. I assumed it was for bodily waste needs, but at this point, having nothing to dispose of, it seemed purposeless. Panic filled me when I heard the rattle of keys outside the steel door and voices whispering. This is it, Linda, time to meet your demise . . .

A powerful voice with an accent that I was unfamiliar with came through the door demanding that I move to the far end of the wall by the cot and turn facing the wall. Why do I have to turn around and face the wall if you're coming to kill me? Who am I going to share this adventure with, earthworms in my grave? Now I know my brain and I do not share my body at the same time because only an airhead at a time like this would think of something so stupid. Should I ask my captors what wall? There are four of them, and two by the cot. Linda, stop your deranged thinking and just find a wall that does not face the door. I heard the door creak open, and the same voice continued to shout demands at me. I faced the wall as I was told, not turning around until the door has been closed again. I followed his instructions to the letter. No one uttered a sound once the door did open, but I did hear the sound of metal clanking on the floor and soon thereafter the sound of the door closing shut, and keys in the tumbler turning the steel door locked again.

Much to my surprise there was a serving dish of food, and just from the smell, I became nauseated due to the fact I had not eaten it seemed for years. I approached the tray very carefully trying to gather my sense of smell to ascertain what could be under this tray. Smothered snakeskin, grilled goat gizzards? People do not kidnap someone and leave him or her sired filet mignon, but what was that aroma arising from under the metal-covered tray? It did not smell like pig slop, or anything from a reptile descent. Slowly lifting the tray from a kneeling position, so I could jump back quickly if need be; I found to my delight a medium rare prime rib with baked potato, and asparagus. There was a side Caesar salad with a warm roll, with a small pat of butter, plastic utensils, and paper napkins. On the floor to the right of the steel door stood a gallon of water and a large plastic cup. Whoever kidnapped me was not poor, so I know money is not the motive for my captivity. I looked at the tray of food again and reasoned I can do one of two things: die from hunger or die from being poisoned. I chose the latter, to eat regardless of the circumstance and the way things were looking. I may as well die with a full stomach. What do these people really want of me? I began to eat slowly.

It was all that I could do to keep myself from choking even as slowly as I ate, not knowing when my next meal would be or if I would even be dead, never to receive another. I thought even prisoners on death row were able to order their last meal of their choice. I just know that Charles and Ciania have been reached by now and are delivering the money at any moment. I also know that many things can go wrong with kidnappings. God, I thought things would be better and simpler when I had no more money issue to contend with. I know that it's not me they wanted; nobody ever kidnapped me when I was poor and threw me in a dark room, and called my boss to deliver one hundred all-meat pizzas or the waitress gets it! This train of thought was only an attempt to keep my spirits up. I knew it was not I they wanted, or money. It was the company, Kusta'ma Kare. I found myself in turmoil again as a result of this company I created with the sole purpose to try to make a difference. It has made a difference all right—of the disastrous kind. This company will be the death of me or the strength of me. Once again, I chose to think the latter.

Later that night, (I guess it was night or just a very long day), I lay upon a very lumpy cot attempting to find sleep but was too scared to do so. Doesn't poison work faster when you are asleep? There you go again, Linda, brain-dead. Before I knew it, I was asleep. If they come in to kill me, at least I won't know about it!

Surprisingly so, I did not wake up dead, meaning that I was surprised that I awoke at all! What should have killed me was this cot I slept on, and not the food. Still very sore, I slung my legs to floor. I could not surmise just how long I had really slept, for a day or just a few hours. What I did find is another tray of food in the center of the floor. I did not hear the sound of anyone coming in or leaving the room or the clanging of the metal door. I guess if one meal did not kill me, then I guess the second will not either. If I did not know when it arrived or how long I've been asleep, then there's no telling how long it has been there. My only wish now is that I had something to wash up with. It has been days since water has touched this face, and my mouth has gone foul from lack of oral hygiene. My kidnappers who are only going to kill me would have no need to wash me up to die.

On the third day I think it was, I was brought a pail of water and soap. I would bath myself first and then wash different items of clothing and dry over the bottom railing of the cot to dry, never being totally undressed at any given time.

Making my way over to the tray, it revealed a wonderful breakfast fit for a queen on a diet. I ate with haste as if once again it may be my last meal, and sleep came again.

I woke up still unaware of the length of time that I had been asleep and just how many days I have been in captivity—four days, five, who knows. My kidnappers and Kusta'ma Kare are the only ones who knew, but I had no idea how long or how long I am to remain.

The eating and sleeping continued with the same routine; far end of the wall in and out, no one asking questions of me at all. What I did continue to do was to check that leviathan of a door every day, and every day it would be locked solid non-budging. I had to continue to check. I believe it was the only thing that kept me from killing myself—the off chance that one day it would swing open, or one day they would leave it open after my ransom had been paid. It would be funny to find that they had left the door unlocked once they had been paid and I never heard the key turn because I was asleep. One must always keep hope alive. And at this point if I did not have anything to hope for, I would find the highest end of this cot and jump off! Well, that thought just shows how much I really wanted to die. Next thought!

I am now certain it has been about a week. Same routine: sleep in and sleep out because I still cannot count the days. But I can tell by the meals now what part of the day it was, and I have had eight breakfasts, eight lunches, and seven dinners. I can hear sound from time to time and voices, and now I do know the voices and the same—two every time. What in the world is taking them so long to kill me or for Kusta'ma Kare to pay them?

I know now that I have been here for at least eight or nine days. It only took seven days to create the earth depending on your belief system or what book you're reading. I chose to think that I have been in here for seven days, meaning I should have been dead or out of here in four. Something is not right! Is Kusta'ma Kare refusing to pay the money? I have signed documents and provided enough money in the event of my abduction, not to waver, and pay on demand. Now that I think about it, if the demand was not met, then surely I would already be dead. This experience should already be over one way or the other. Why has it not ended?

"Charles, are you saying pay the money?" Karen asked.

"We have no choice," Charles replied.

"That is and always has been Linda's request, and we all know that. But what if we pay the money and she is already dead? That phone call came three days ago with demand to pay up in five days. We have two days left."

"If we don't pay the money, she surely dies," Charles said.

"I have no choice. Ciania and I will get the money and make the exchange. I am surprised that they did not ask for more than one million dollars, it could just be a distraction asking for such a small amount of money. Anybody that reads the newspapers or watches television in any language has to know what Linda and Kusta'ma Kare is worth." On that note, there was nothing that anyone could say to stop Charles; he would get Linda back if it meant selling the whole company assets now worth billions in any legal tender. Ciania and Charles left for their private offices linked to Linda's.

Charles did not have to go far, there was a floor safe under his desk. Paying the ransom was not an option for him; it has now become his mission. My God, Charles thought to himself, what will I do without her? Have these people lost their entire mind? I will search the entire universe until she is returned to me and they better pray to their God that she is not hurt or harmed in any way. Charles entered the combination to the safe and counted out the money needed that was demanded for Linda's release; he counted it in one-hundred-thousand-dollar stacks.

Charles had everyone but Ciania under the impression that he had to fly to a different location to obtain the resources for Linda's release. Ciania and he were the only two who knew all the locations where the secured money was located. Linda herself did not know all the locations just in case she was forced to locate the money while held under duress. Charles finished counting and stacking the money in various bundles and closed his secured briefcase.

Charles picked up the phone and called Ciania. "Ciania, I need you to come to my office right away." When Ciania entered Charles's office, he was sitting at his desk, elbows on the desk with his head in his hands. She had never seen him in such a state. When is he going to admit to himself and to her that he loves her?

"Yes, Charles, I am here," Ciania said.

"Ciania, I am going to need your help with the delivery. I make the exchange; I need you to be my driver and my eyes and ears."

"No problem," Ciania said, "is that all you need me to do?"

"Yes," Charles said.

"Charles, are you going to be all right? You know that I will do everything within my power, and I have the arsenal packed and ready to go."

"Then we are going to need more than what you have in your office or at home if they have harmed her, but right now none," Charles spouted.

"I know, Ciania," added Charles, "but we will not be taking any firearms."

"What?" Ciania replied, "what are we going to take, a fruit basket and roses? Charles, I know that you are under a lot of stress and pressure right now, but have you really given thought to going without any protection? Not just for our protection but to go get Linda in case things get worse. You know, something like where is the money and here is the location where you can pick up Linda. I know that we are not going to leave with just an address and no money. Charles, I am talking about that kind of worst case."

"Charles," Ciania said, "I have to let you know that we did agree to pay the money if anything ever happened to Linda. The money doesn't bother me because I always knew that's what we agreed to do. What does bother me is the fact that these people think that they can call up like ordering a takeout and get it. Who's to say they just won't kidnap her once a year when money is low? I say we go in strongly armed, kill them, and get her!" "Get her from where, Ciania?" Charles screamed, "Ciania, stop!"

"I know how you feel about Linda, and that she is your very best friend but what I need you to do now is understand. I do not need this right now. We are going unarmed and with no fruit basket, no roses, and no guns. What I do want to do is make sure that we follow their demands to the letter. I do not want anything to go wrong, and I don't want to find out later that you took one."

"And if it does?" Ciania said, "something goes wrong?"

"Ciania, just make sure on our part that it does not."

"Now here is the rest of the instruction that came in on my private line. Just how they got my number, I do not know."

"Maybe Linda was forced to give it to them," Charles said, "but I have a gut feeling that Linda offered up that information without any hesitation or duress. Linda probably shouted out every number she knew until someone listened to her, saying that we would pay anything they wanted for her release. You know how Linda is; she is talking her head off at this moment."

"Ciania, that will be all for now," Charles said, "we will meet here in my office at eight o'clock tomorrow night. The pickup is at midnight, and I want you and I to go over the last-minute details. I feel that we should use your car, it is faster than any of our company cars are. Make sure the car is serviced to the hilt."

"I know," Charles said, holding his right hand up as to keep Ciania from speaking, "you keep that Corvette of yours in mint condition, but I want everything running smoothly, even that prize of a car of yours."

I heard noise on the other side of the door for the first time. This time the voices were saying other things, other than step back and face the wall. By this time, I knew the voices although I did not understand the language. Their English was always broken when they ordered me around. But right now, they are speaking in their native tongue. Voices raised and angered. I couldn't understand that much, but I wish I knew what they were arguing about. I walked closer to the door in case my native language slipped from their tongue, and then maybe I could get a handle on what was going on around here. I just knew it was about me; they would not be arguing about what to order for dinner. I heard the key in the turn lock to my left. I have been paying close attention to that door every day. When it turns to my left it is opening, and when it turns to my right it is locking. Why I stored that information I am unsure. The lock turns one way and then the other like they were going to enter and then locked the door back and changed their mind. Were they coming to release me or kill me? That's the first time I heard them at the door without them demanding my regular position before they entered. Maybe I shouldn't be in such urgency for them to open the door until I knew exactly what they had words about.

There is already a tray of food set out that they brought containing a tuna and rye sandwich. How ironic or symbolic. Now that I know it is lunchtime and midday, I also know that I have been here now I figure a little over a week give or take a day.

I was eating the sandwich I never got a chance to eat the day I was kidnapped, and I could tell it was from the same deli. I wondered what all this could mean, tuna and rye, arguing it's all too much for me. They're not going to have to kill me; if I keep this up, I will die from worrying. Sometimes things are out of our control, I thought, and this would be one of those times. Time to take a nap. Before I laid down, I glanced at the door again, and the lock position was to my right. It was locked. Every day, I would check the position of the keyhole. It was easier than leaning up against the huge door. It was locked. I slept.

Waking up, I remembered it being the best night sleep I have had since being here. I still cannot (for the life of me) figure out what type of room this is. Just because it is dark does not make it is a basement. I do not I believe I slept long enough the first night to be in England or some far-off country, so I know that it's not a dungeon. I also know that I cannot be far, when you eat a sandwich from your favorite deli, you know it, or they drove hundreds of miles to get it, which I doubt. I could be aboveground, or below ground or even on ground level; it just doesn't have any windows. What was peculiar was that everything was so evenly square, almost as if the room was designed for this purpose. Nothing here had been boarded up are altered. Everything was smooth and gray, even in color. The clammy feeling I had the first night came from an overhead pipe running the length of the room made of steel just like its brother (the door), and a little moisture from time to time gathered on the outside—air-conditioner system I thought. The first night I was here, the overhead light was not on, but over the days I have been paying more attention to details of every corner of my prison. The room was only about eleven by nine feet, thank God any smaller than that and I would have died for sure. There was not a ventilation system, so I am glad that my waste container was emptied twice a day, when they brought breakfast and the last meal at dinner.

The more I studied my tomb; the more I noticed the room was too perfect—almost like a square painted box. It had to be something before it became what it was now, a room for captivity. But what? The floor had the same surface as the walls, and the ceiling was smooth and hard not like steel, or metal but like a hard rubber or plastic. How odd. Who would build a room with the sole purpose of storing hostages, unless this was full-time employment and they had it built. I guess they only kidnapped people in the United States or locally unless there were hundreds of places like this one all over the world. This place was still odd nonetheless. Almost like something out of the movies.

No sooner that I had that thought than I saw the keyhole turn to my left.

"Back up and face the far wall," I heard one of the two familiar voices say.

It must be dinner time. As always I followed my captors' instructions. This time it took a little longer for me to hear the door close. When I turned around, there was indeed a tray with food in the middle of the floor, but what took so long for them to leave it? The sound of their voice came again in a higher rage than before from the other side of the door. I heard their voice fade away. For the first time, I never glanced at the keyhole.

I was a little hungry, so I began to eat, and before I knew it, I feel asleep. For some reason other than being a prisoner for over a week, I could not sleep and could not wake up either as if I were drugged. Is that why they were in the room longer than normal? Did they put something in my food? Sit up, I told myself, but I could not; I fell hard asleep.

"Ciania, what time do you have?" Charles asked.

"It is a little after ten o'clock. I have gone over the checklist three times, and I have driven the pickup route four times."

Ciania replied, "Charles, I don't think we can be any more prepared than we are now—" Before Ciania could finish, the phone on Charles's desk rung. Charles and Ciania looked at one another simultaneously.

Ciania asked Charles, "Who could be calling that line at this time of night?" Charles caught the phone on the second ring, his voice firm and secure. "This is Charles, can I help you?" The voice one the other side of the line said, "The time has been moved up to eleven o'clock; be ready, and I don't want any excuses."

Charles lost his composure as he said, "I want to talk to Linda first before the meet."

"You are in no position to spout orders, Mr. Edwards," the voice said on the other end of the line.

Charles's angrily replied, "Yes, I am, matter of fact I am the only person in position to give you what you want at this minute, and if Linda is already dead, then it seems absurd don't you think, to even show up with the money. What you don't want to do is mistake me for an attorney at this moment and not a man that is set on getting Ms. Nalley back."

Charles continued, "You have only twenty minutes to get Ms. Nalley to the phone, or get a phone to Ms. Nalley, or the meeting is off." With that said, Charles hung up the phone.

Ciania had only seen Charles like that twice since she had known them, and if these kidnappers did not fulfill his demands, there would be no meeting, no drop-off money, and possibly no Linda.

I was finally able to wake from that deadly sleep I had fell in. Still somewhat under the influence of something, I poured myself a small amount of water, taking a deep breath. I notice the door; why my attention was focused on the door at that moment only God himself knew. The locking position of the keyhole was to my advantage—it was turned to my left, unlocked. Not believing my eyes or if my mind was transmitting the information correctly, I rubbed my eyes and looked again. I reached for all the clothing that I had, pulling myself together quickly, then stopped. Where am I going if the door is open? How do I know there is not another type of dead bolt on the outside? As if a force was guiding me not to worry about anything until I had to, that must be what that adage means—"cross that bridge when you get to it" meant off to the door with whatever I had on leaving everything else behind.

Charles and Ciania both continued to look at their watches almost every minute, staring at the phone. No call yet and ten minutes had gone by.

Getting to the door, all I could do was to look to the heavens and say, "here I go, ready or not." I slowly leaned on the door.

"Ciania, would you stop pacing the floor," Charles said.

"Well its pace the floor or jump out the window, which one do you want me to do?" Ciania snapped.

"Neither," Charles yelled, "I just want some stillness so I can hear the phone ring. What am I saying?"

"Ciania, you cannot jump out the window. If you do, who is going to drive me to pick up Linda?" Charles said.

"I know," Ciania said, "we are both on edge right now, I understand I'll jump out the window if the phone does not ring."

The door swung open. I stood frozen with disbelief. Should I step out the door or just stand here? I often lay on that cot and stared at this door, wanting, wishing, and praying it would open. Now that it has, what should I do? That same force beckoned me to continue. Continue where, which way? Come on, brain, now is not the time to be an absent member of my body.

Only one more minute had passed, but to Charles it felt like an eternity.

"Charles, if you pick up that phone one more time to see if it's working, the kidnappers may call and won't be able to get through."

"The phone is working," Ciania said, "now please put it down."

Go to the right, Linda, I told myself, you can never go wrong going to the right. To my right I went, but before I ventured too far I turned around and quietly pushed the door close. Maybe if this location is monitored from somewhere else, they will not know that I have gone until they actually entered the room. I turned in flight as if on fire.

It was hard to see my surroundings due to the darkness and the effect of whatever they had given me as a sedative. Then

I stopped again with disbelief. I could see a dim light ahead, but ahead of what? I continued toward the light and tripped over something and fell. Okay, Linda, do not be a movie cliché running from the monster and trip and fall. Get up, I told myself, but not only that, what did I trip over?

Charles was sitting at his desk, Ciania on the other side. Twenty minutes had almost passed by. Only eight minutes left before that phone should and better be ringing off the hook with Linda's voice on the other end if only for a short second, Charles thought to himself. He dare not repeat that thought to Ciania.

I stood to see what I had tripped and fell over; it was . . . electric wires? Thick cords of them neatly bundled together right in the middle of what, where am I? I didn't feel enclosed anymore like I was in huge room. Where was that light coming from? I clung to the wall to the right of the door, but when the wall wrapped in a different direction instead of what I thought should be forward, I stood still again, not wanting to trip over anything else. Somehow, I have to find my way over to that light. I followed the direction of the light, proceeding slowly.

The light appeared to be hanging in midair surrounded by vast darkness. I'll just go in the direction of the light in hopes not trip and fall. I'll go slowly.

"Ciania, I believe it has been long enough unless they or he is waiting until the twenty-minute mark to call," Charles said, "unless . . ."

"Don't unless me," Ciania said to Charles, "I don't want to even think along those lines. I know what you're thinking now, Charles; if Linda was still alive, they or he would have called back by now."

"You're right," Charles said, "no Linda, then no phone call; so what will be their next move, or better yet, what will be ours?"

"Now I'm thinking that I should have called the police like the other board members wanted me to do."

"Charles, this is not the time to second-guess yourself," Ciania said, "who knew how the events would unfold? All we can do for now is wait."

I finally located the source of the light. It was suspended from a high ceiling right above and the entrance looks like that of a hangar door for airplanes. Great, I thought another huge door, now how long do I have to wait for this one to open? I guided my hands around the immediate area by the door to look for a switch of some sort; if there was one light, then there has to be another.

I found what I was looking for. I flipped the switch upward, and the surrounding lit up like Christmas lights everywhere. At that moment as my eyes took in the interior of my confines, it all made sense. A room for imprisonment too perfect, like made to hold hostages, and that it was.

"I hate to tell you, Charles," Ciania said, "but are you aware that it is well past the time of our awaited call?" Charles could only reply, "I know."

"What are we going to do now?" Ciania asked.

"Wait," Charles said, "wait, that's all we can do for now, wait."

Looking around the room (to my surprise but unsurprised at the same time), I took in the room in which I was standing, and props were all around me. Stage lighting, backdrops, miniature buildings, what was all this? I was either standing in a movie studio, or a theater. That's why the room was so perfectly made to order. I walked around and saw more and more of stage like settings. I was standing in front of a barn with the whole front missing, made for filming with hay, pitchforks, pigs and stuffed cows. To my right was a desert setting fully stocked with stuffed camels and fake cactuses. To my left was a Western town; my next thought was how far away from the office I really was, and were there any studios near the office. Of course, I would not know that because I didn't drive around a lot in Eureka to really know what was around every corner. What I did know was that I have got to get out of here, but first I have to do one more thing . . . .

"Charles, what are we going to do? They are now an hour later calling," Ciania said. Charles hung his head and said nothing.

Looking around for something to jam the door lock with, I needed as much time as possible before they found I had escaped, and not in their made-to-order prison.

"I am calling the FBI," Ciania said, reaching for the phone. Charles grabbed the phone from Ciania. "Ciania, what are you going to say to the FBI? That we were getting ready to pay some kidnappers that didn't call back? Hang up the phone, Ciania," Charles said.

I spotted a tubing of liquid cement on the floor by an army barrack. Now all I need was something small enough to insert just a dab into the key lock. Is this my lucky day or what? Sitting on desk in the barracks was a pair of reading glasses. Breaking them in half, I went running. The room was big enough and lit up well enough for me to see. As I came closer to the door where I not long ago escaped, I slowed down listening for any voices or noise. I heard none. Dead silence. Hiding behind a stuffed camel, I unscrewed the tube of cement spreading a small dab on the end of the horn-rimmed frame glasses and crept around the camel. I knelt down, slowly sticking the tip of the glasses with the liquid cement on the end in the keyhole. That's it; just enough for the key not to go in but not enough for them to see why, I squeezed the remainder inside the cavity of the lock. Hope this stuff dries fast.

"Charles, how long are we going to wait before we do something?" Ciania asked.

"Do something, like what?" Charles replied.

Reaching the door where the huge light hung, I tried the latch, and the door opened. Some kidnappers, I thought to myself, but I guess they never figured I would get this far. I reached back inside the door and turned off the light switch, putting the movie set back to sleep.

Once again to my right, I went and found myself in the inner city, just one block down a dark alley. How could that be, with no one seeing me enter. At this point who cares? It must have been late in the night; there were no cars or cabs. I stayed close in the shadows instead of the street lights since I had no idea where my kidnappers were, and I did not want to risk being kidnapped again trying to escape.

Thank God for always going to the right. Twenty minutes later, there it was; the first thing I saw was the deli where it all started and Kusta'ma Kare towering, calling me home. Not more that three short blocks away and across the street from where I stood was a phone booth. I opted to use the phone for someone to get me, and I stayed in the shadows until they arrived.

Charles jumped out of his chair when the phone rung, knocking it off its cradle before saying, "Where the . . ." but before Charles could finish his question, an operator said, "Would you accept a collect call from Linda Nalley?"

Charles dropped the phone, "Charles, Charles, what's the matter?" Ciania shouted, "did something happen to Linda?" Charles could not believe his ears they had her call collect, and his next thought was whether this was some kind of joke. Never replying to Ciania, he reached for the receiver that had blundered on his desk, replied to the operator, "Yes, I will."

I gave an account of my activities as I could recall them for two days of briefing from members of my board. My seldom-speaking brother stood and said, "Linda, exactly what are we to do with this information? You know the location from where you escape and refuse to disclose that information with us. Why?"

"John, my brother, I love you, I love you all, and I am certain that my disappearance has upset you all greatly. I want all of you to understand that what I say now I have given great consideration too. I will not take anyone or revisit my place of captivity." Reasoning to myself this morning when I woke up in my own bed, I looked at the heavens and thanked God that I did not wake up in that solitary room. I woke up this morning and thanked God that I escaped unharmed, and in doing so made my decision not to go back but to look forward in the blessing and not harbor the circumstance of my past. One cannot be thankful and vengeful in one breath. If you're vengeful, you are not thankful, and thankful I am. No more was said on the subject as we all glanced at each other individually in silence.

The kidnappers on the other hand were cursing each other out in a language I don't believe either understood or blaming the other for jamming the lock on the door, still unaware at that moment I was not inside their custom built room for captivity.

Acceptance

IT HAD BEEN almost six years that Kusta'ma Kare was up and operational. I'm not really sure when it all happened, and trust me, it did not happen overnight. After all the screaming and yelling, lawsuits, refusal to pay, people got ruder before they got better. There were breakouts in groceries stores and gas station, and people were filled with more bitterness than ever before. Once again, I was filled with the dread of hopelessness. I thought Kusta'ma Kare was to bring about betterment of people. There was hatred at a level I had never seen before. What to do now? My heart saddens as day-to-day events unfolded. Once again, I looked to the heavens and Mr. Jacobs for answers. Once again the answer came to me. Transformation of thought brought clear skies after the storm. All types of clichés came to me. What did not cross my mind at the time with all the dread was the thought of giving up. With all the sadness, somehow I knew not to give up. I've come too far not to see this through, even after the kidnapping. For the first time in a long time, my mind was clear as a bell; and for it to be clear as a bell, it had to be present sharing the same time and space, not somewhere in the future trying to lure me forward. The oneness of it all is, I believe, called a moment of clarity. One with the universal balance of things, no wonder when people would say my mind is clear. Clear! Free of clutter, confusions, and indecisiveness. I get it now! I guess all this time my mind knew where I was to travel and how to make the journey to get there. Sometimes, one must journey through the hardest times of their lives to find the relevance of things. I was no longer wandering in a maze of indecisiveness, and my mind was present and in full control without the resistance of my body. Both in unison, mind and body pushed forward toward the goal that my life was intended. I was never the type who believed that destiny's road is already paved for one to follow, but now I know this was and is my destiny. And people do cross your path for reasons and seasons.

Thank you, Mr. Jacobs. Now in the moment, I thanked God for my old job of serving pizza, an experience that encouraged me to want a sit-down job that led to customer service in the telecommunication field that led to Mr. Jacobs, that led to this moment in time with mind and body as one! Whew! What a journey! Now it is time to get on with the business of getting on with life. I can only change myself, and the moment I stopped being a victim of my own circumstances is when my circumstance changed.

Mr. Jacobs, I will continue to be kind no matter what my circumstance; I will continue to treat my employees, loved ones, and friends with mutual respect; the world will not get what the world does not get. I have also found that people cannot want more for others anything; that they do not want for themselves. What I do know is that if we do not change as a people, as a whole, we will diminish with nothing to bind us. With common courtesies gone, with human kindness relinquished, we are no more than robots going through the motions. Mr. Jacobs, my optimistic goal was that somehow as people would could customer care everyone every day. Spouse, children, coworkers, employees, employers, field workers, everyone no matter what. Basic respect for humanity was simple I thought, but it is not so simply done. Thinking my last silent thoughts to Mr. Jacobs, I would give Kusta'ma Kare a few more years and then step down. The failure is not in the attempt; the failure is in the not trying. I tried, and with that last thought, the next thought was to get on with Kusta'ma Kare business, my business, the one I think Mr. Jacobs would be very proud of.

The very next morning, lying in bed, I read my favorite newspaper the *Wall Street Journal*. There it was, the name of Kusta'ma Kare splashed across the front page telling about an unbelievable rise in the stock market for big business. Independent companies had closed their doors and cannot compete with the impeccable rising business of Kusta'ma Kare and other big business that have adopted the Kusta'ma Kare way. The article went on to state that at the end of the trading day, a new stock record had been broken. It was less than twenty-four hours when my resolve was not to worry about the condition of the world and the people that lived in it and only do what I myself could do to be a better person. And as soon as I let go of the responsibility to change the world and only change myself did it happen. Things changed.

I quickly got dressed and ran to the corner market and bought several newspapers, and there it was! I stood there with tears in my eyes as I glanced from headline to headline. Kusta'ma Kare was this and Kusta'ma Kare was that. Other major companies across the world are patterning their businesses with the motto "hire the best, pay the best, and you will get the best!" Standing in disbelief, I scrambled for my cell phone in my bag to call Charles. Two rings and he said, "Linda, have you seen the news this morning? It is amazing! Honey, you did it, it's all over the news!" Charles said.

Honey? Did Charles just call me honey? Maybe he was too electrified by the news and did not realize what he was saying, or maybe he did. Charles and I talked until my battery went dead on my cell phone. The last thing I remember saying was "Charles, can you hear me now?"

I went back to my penthouse to give my head a chance to stop whirling. I would call Charles back in a minute. Well, needless to say, I slept the rest of the night. This was the first night since I can remember that I did not toss and turn from one side to another. What I did find strange when I reached to rub my back and stretched was that it was gone—not my back but the eerie feeling that had been creeping up my back for so long. Completely gone; no knot, no tension, no eerie feeling. As I went throughout that day, I would stop from time to time in stillness checking for eerie feeling signs. None came.

At 7:00 a.m. Charles called. "Linda, I tried to call you all night, are you all right?" Charles said.

"Yes, Charles." I said I am. "I'm so sorry. After I lost your call, I came home lying down for only a second with the intent to call, and I woke this morning still fully dressed. Did I dream yesterday's news events?" I asked.

"No, you did not," Charles said, "it is still running on all channels this morning, special reports and all. Congratulations, Linda, your dream for your vision of Kusta'ma Kare has come true. The news reports also stated that people are coming to work on time, being gracious and kind. There was another report ran on your company, a survey of how people felt about Kusta'ma Kare. You won hands down, your employees love you and Kusta'ma Kare."

Charles and Linda

ON YEAR NINE, the phone rang at 4:00 a.m. "Linda, wake up! This is Charles."

"Charles, you called on the number only you have. I know that it is you; what is wrong and do you know what time it is?"

"Yes, I looked at the clock before I called, I am well aware of what time it is."

"Okay, now that we are both aware of the time, Charles, what is it that could not wait until the sun rose?"

"Linda, we need to talk."

"Charles, we are talking," I said, "what is the matter, are you all right?"

"Yes, I am fine, thanks for asking, but what I have to say I do not think it's best to say over the phone."

"Then, Charles, why didn't you wait until we were in person to say it? You're confusing me. Well? I am waiting."

"Linda, Kusta'ma Kare is doing well now and you have more money than you could spend in fifty lifetimes and . . ."

"Yes, Charles, I'm waiting. You are making me nervous."

"Linda, I have reserved a table at your favorite restaurant for nine tomorrow night so we can talk. Please, if your calendar is full, will you clear it?" I thought to myself that was not a request; that was a statement that left room for no excuses.

"Yes, Charles, but I do not understand."

"Linda, please, no more questions."

"Okay, okay, Charles, I will be there at eight forty-five."

"Nine o'clock, Linda, you will be shown right to our table." Charles said a very soft good night.

That's it, now I can't go back to sleep, I thought. I know that Charles has been acting different lately. Distracted most time when we would be going over business details, but what this is about I have no idea. Is he going to tell me that it is time for him to move on? That's it, for the last nine years, Charles had dedicate his whole life to the company and to me.

The poor man has had no private life; how selfish of me. It was always Charles this and Charles that, fly here, sign this, approve that. It's a wonder he had not left me long ago. What am I going to do without him? I guess I would soon find out. For the duration of the morning I decide to brew coffee while practicing how to be gracious when Charles breaks the news to me that he is moving on and not break down in tears and faint again for the second time in my life with life-changing events. Well I guess I knew that the time would come, and I am in fact surprised that it took this long for it to come. Pouring a cup of hot steaming coffee, I wondered where I would find another attorney and friend all wrapped in one. There I go again being selfish instead of wishing him the best and wondering who the woman lucky and blessed enough to have him would be. With a silent prayer to myself for his well-being and future endeavors, I left to kitchen to take a shower.

After showering and dressing for the office, I decided to call and ask Barbara to take care of a few calendar events that I had set for the day I would call later. As hard as I tried, I could not concentrate on anything but tonight's dinner and my demise. I dressed in a casual dress and flats and made up my mind to go shopping. Maybe I would buy a new sexy black dress. A black dress is appropriate for mourning, and low cut to keep his mind off leaving me. What am I saying, leaving me? He is not with me; he is with the company. I am acting as if we are getting ready to sign our divorce papers. Today has been the second longest day of my life; the reading of the will was the first. I called for the limousine to meet me out front in thirty minutes.

By one o'clock that afternoon, I had finished all my shopping. I bought a sexy black dress by a new Italian designer; low cut in the front, and cut all the way to the to the legal area of my back with out being arrested for indecent exposure. I also bought a sexy black three-inch pump with black sheer hose, handwoven from French silkworms. Wow, Linda, do you think you bought enough black? Charles is going to ask who died or if you attended a funeral prior to dinner.

Looking at the time, there are still too many hours remaining in the day to contend with, so off I went to get a facial, manicure, and pedicure. At four o'clock in the afternoon there was still too much time on my hands. I took myself to lunch for a small salad. I did not want to spoil my meal for tonight. Tonight! I wonder what time at dinner he will break the news; probably after dinner like fattening up the livestock before the kill. Eat your salad, Linda, I thought to myself worried about tonight.

After all the shopping and grooming, I still did not feel any better; it is still only six thirty. What to do now? Wait until tonight was all that I could do. I took the limousine back to my suite for a bubble bath and a short nap, since I did not get that much sleep last night, and attempt to get some now. It still may be futile, but I will try. I don't want to show up tired looking and worried.

Napped I did. At dinner, I showed up promptly at nine o'clock. As promised, I was showed to my table by a waiter, which assured me that Mr. Edwards had called announcing his arrival time in about two minutes. I ordered seltzer water with lime while I waited.

Charles showed up in a dark brown suit and white shirt with tie, this was for sure a business meeting; it's a wonder that he did not bring his attorney. That's funny, I guess really rich and powerful attorneys still need someone to defend and manage their affairs. No attorney accompanied him; he was alone, and for the first time in a long time, I felt alone.

"Linda, thanks for coming on so short notice."

Charles was more professional than he should be addressing me at dinner, but my rebuttal was professional as well.

"You're welcome, Charles, not a problem." I started to go straight for the throat and ask what all this was about but restrained from continuing on that line of thought.

Charles seated himself, and we were brought menus. Charles ordered a small shrimp cocktail; I ordered crab cakes grilled and served with a butter sauce. I did not want this dinner to last too long so I could get to the business at hand. By the end of dinner, over coffee Charles said, "Linda . . ."

I sat straight up in bed to find I was only dreaming, and whatever news Charles had to share, I had awaken before I knew just what it was. Thank God, I didn't have to experience that emotion twice even while sleeping. I leaned over and looked at the clock;

it was seven fifteen. Yips! I overslept. The restaurant was at least thirty to forty minutes drive across town depending on traffic. I am going to be late.

I rush around to get dressed like Cinderella for the ball; it actuality may be more like Cinderella after the ball losing her Prince Charming. I quickly reached for the phone and called Ciania.

"Ciania, I need you."

"What is the matter? Are you hurt? You sound frantic."

"No, nothing like you think, but I do need you here with the limo at eight o'clock. I will meet you downstairs," Ciania agreed and hung up. I could have driven myself, but just in case Ciania has to commit me to an asylum after dinner I better have her drive.

I hurried to dress and took another shower. At seven forty-five, I touched up my makeup and grabbed the keys and purse. Since I don't smoke or drink, I was a nervous wreck. Like clockwork, Ciania was as always on time. Ciania greeted me and opened the back to the limousine door.

"Where to?" she said.

"Ray's Seafood Restaurant on the pier. I have to be there at nine sharp." Ciania looked over her shoulder at me while navigating through town.

"Linda, I know this is none of my business, but if I did not know better I would say that you have a date, but your tone indicates a business dinner, should I be in attendance?

"No, Ciania, I will be fine. What I do need is for you to store Ray's Seafood Restaurant telephone number in your cell/car phone it does not matter. What does matter is that you call inside the restaurant at ten o'clock and ask for me. My cell phone will be off at dinner.

"Yes, Linda, but are you certain that I do not need to be inside with you?"

"Yes, I am sure."

It was ten minutes to nine when we arrived at Ray's Seafood Restaurant. The lot was empty. Charles knew that this was my favorite restaurant. Maybe I should have inquired which one of my favorites. I reached for the phone to call Charles when the front door opened and Ray, the owner, came to the limousine door.

"Linda, how lovely to see you. Your table is ready."

"Ray, it is always a pleasure."

"How is business?" I said.

"Wonderful," he replied, "could not be better, had a full house last night, and my reservation list is two weeks in advance." So my next thought is where is everyone now?

Before going inside, Ciania insisted to know with whom I was having this date or meeting with (or whatever it was). I had already been kidnapped once. I guess she did not want to relive that ordeal by letting me out of her presence. I leaned over and said," I'm suppose to meet Charles here for a business meeting, Ciania, put the mental gun back in the holster! Please, I will be fine."

Ciania watched as I walked through the restaurant doors. I could feel her eyes on the back of my head. I continued to walk inside escorted by the owner, Ray. Once totally inside the foyer, I was escorted the rest of the way. I was still wondering why no one else was present in line or at the other tables. Ray walked me through the restaurant to a private dining room.

I stood totally breathless as my eyes took inventory of the room into which I was to dine and meet Charles. Flowers, flowers, and more flowers everywhere . . . Not just roses, but I believe there was a flower from every state in the union, and some imported. It looked more like a greenhouse in the dining room instead of an eatery. What were the flowers all about? Charles sure had a way of saying good-bye. Ray begun to seat me when I asked the time,

"Ms. Nalley, it is 9:00 p.m. sharp, may I get you something to drink?" Boy if I were a drinker, this would be the perfect time for a scotch on the rocks.

"Seltzer water please, Ray, will be fine with a wage of lime."

"No problem, Ms. Nalley."

"Ray, may I ask, are you short staffed?"

"No, Ms. Nalley, the staff has the night off, and I will serve you and Mr. Edwards personally, and he should be arriving soon." That statement was déjà vu. Great, all I needed was to be left alone in my head until Charles arrived. What was all this about was all I could think about? Ray waiting on us personally, private dining room filled with flowers. "Charles, why couldn't you just say what you had to say over the phone and get it over with?" No sooner than that thought left my mind, Charles walked in dashing in appearance. Charles had the, "I just stepped off a cruise ship look." Charles wore a beige linen suit with no tie, a tan silk shirt with matching low cut loafers, no socks. I stared at his appearance again. I thought to myself that this was not the business attire one would wear when you're getting ready to end a business arrangement. But what do I know? I have never had anyone meet me to end a business arrangement.

As Charles continued toward the table approaching once again as if in slow motion, he leaned over and gave me a kiss on the forehead. That's it, the kiss of death, I thought to myself.

"Good evening, Charles, what a lovely room . . ." Charles seated himself and then asked if my needs had been addressed to my satisfaction and was I ready to see the menu. Ray had a special menu prepared for tonight. Yes, by all means, you may let Ray know that he can bring the menu.

With all the necessities out of the way and dinner eaten, I finally had the nerve to ask what the meeting and dinner was all about.

"Sure, Linda, right after I order the desert." Desert was an understatement as Ray walked in pushing a food cart with something humongous atop.

Ray pushed the cart over to the table and stopped.

"Mr. Edwards, will there be anything else?"

"No," Charles answered, "thank you, Ray, that will be enough, great job."

Charles then looked over at me and said, "Linda . . . I have been in your employ almost ten years, and your friend equally as long. What I do not think you know is that I have been your biggest fan from the day you walked into our offices . . ."

"Yes, Charles," I interrupted.

"Please, Linda, do not disrupt me until I am finished. What I am trying to say is that I have been many things to you but . . ." Charles looked down at his hands for a second, and I have never seen him so humbled. Damn it, Charles, just say good-bye and get it over with, I thought to myself.

"Linda, let's just have desert." Charles stood facing the food cart that Ray had wheeled in and undraped the most beautiful sight I have ever seen in my life. As tears rolled down my eyes, I glanced at what had to have taken hours to design by hand, a sculptured cake in the likeness of him and me three inches high and very lifelike.

Lifelike figurines of the two of us were placed on top of a miniature fifteen-story office building with the name "Kusta'ma Kare" on the building. The image of me was standing, and the image of him bowed on one knee with a tiny little gold-wrapped gift box lifted up in my direction. Charles walked over the tiny gift box and lifted it from the tiny version of himself. Could this mean what I think it does? Charles walked over to me opening the jewelry box, which held a single-cut, ten-carat sparkling yellow diamond set in twenty-four-carat white gold ring. Tears could not stop streaming from my eyes. It's wonderful! I could not see the ring at all clearly for the tears, but I have the rest of my life to look at it. Charles lifted my chin and clearly said, "Life around you, Linda, is like being on top of the world, and I want to know if you would be my wife because I no longer want to be on top of the world; I want to be your world if you would have me." Needless to say, I fainted. I guess he'll take that as a yes?

Sitting up in my chair still in the restaurant, I heard the words "Linda, Linda, are you okay?" I looked up at Charles and Ciania; she was fanning me with a white linen napkin from the dining table saying, "Linda, breathe." Finally, once again I remembered why I fainted. I looked around to see if I was dreaming again and if Charles and that beautiful cake were still in the room. Yes, they were; it was not a dream. Charles was standing next to the cake behind Ciania.

"Linda, I love you very much. Please don't die on me now."
Charles smiled.

The next thing I knew and can clearly remember was
making an appointment with the wedding planner. Wow, wedding
planner. I would have never thought that day would come that I
have dreamed of so often. Now that the time has arrived, Linda,
think about it. What do you and Charles really have in common but
the business? What do the two of us, as a couple, enjoy together?
What, what, what? Linda, stop sabotaging your marriage before
it even happens! The one thing I do know is that this is true love,
and what he likes, I will learn to like and love. There will be some
things that we find we love together. Although people make life
and relationships difficult; they truly are not. The wedding of all
weddings went off without a hitch.

Jason was still attending college abroad studying for his
master's various majors, still unsure of what his career choice
would be. But he had stated he wanted to be well diverse. Jason was
beyond doubt like his father and has extremely strong character,
good qualities, strong sense of right and wrong in life, and morals
that are unsurpassed. So with Jason well on his way as a young
man and getting a good education, Charles had no worries for his
son's future.

Charles and I have discussed on occasion when we would sell the business to take one of our yachts and sail for about a year around the world. All aboard . . . one captain, one first mate, and one cook

Over the years, I did learn that whenever Charles did take time away from the business, he would be on one of our smaller company boats and fish in salt waters. I guess that will be something I will learn to like. I do love the open waters and the vastness of it all. Maybe it will be one of those things I will learn to love. I wonder how many things he will have to learn to love and like about me. If one is willing, one can adapt to anything, I say.

Time to Sell

ON YEAR TEN, taxes started to go way down as big business adapted to hire the best and pay the best following Kusta'ma Kare policy. Smaller business were paying higher wages for the task in life that didn't require carrying briefcases. One could now flip a burger and support their family with pride. Employees were able to pay for medical expenses without government-assisted programs. Single parents were able to afford child care without financial assistance. People, it seemed, as a whole, were happy again. More people were able to pay their bills on time with less stress. Less stress meant happy people; happy people meant happy employees; happy employees meant less people calling in. With less absences from work, there was more productivity; productivity produced better business growth. Better business growth meant increased revenue. Schools had reported better grades and attendances, fewer children calling in sick, as a direct result of proper medical care and better meals being cooked at home. A two family income was no longer required. Moms that chose to stay home, were not financially forced to seek employment to support a normal dinner and a movie lifestyle. Yes, God, I would say that things were better all around. Not just betterment of people but betterment of lifestyles as well, a quality of life that one could be proud of. Ten long years, and the result of the vision had a better effect on the world than I could have ever imagined. I guess when you have betterment of people and human nature, it creates a domino effect. I could not have foreseen the economy as a whole reaping the benefit of a simple vision I had only ten years ago.

Mr. Jacobs, I hope what they say about heaven is true, but somehow I know that it is because I feel your presence even now and your approval. How did you know what turn of events would unfold by adding one name to your last will and testament? But you must have had an idea. If the world only knew, it all started with a nine-minute phone call. Thank you, Mr. Jacobs, for changing so many lives, and not just mine.

A time to sell, I thought to myself one day while reviewing the company financial records. The business had done well, I must say, and employees were happy, which was my main concern. Kusta'ma Kare Christmas bonuses, child care on site, minor shopping conveniences so employees don't have to spend gas to go five miles to the corner store. Money I already had, and my joy now was the attendance reports over the years and employees' surveys on how we could improve relations with employees. Over the ten-year span, only five came in and three have been fulfilled. Employees at all levels were satisfied.

Charles and I have spoken often about selling the business due to the fact that we are so happy being happy that most time the business seemed to always be on the bottom of the to-do list. We have been married for over a year now, and the business was running almost on autopilot. The main problem we were having was who to sell the business to. It had to be someone who shared the same concept on life that he and I share, or what would be the point? It would undo everything I strived and worked for. Stockholders would have to be on the same accord, or finding another single individual with the same dreams and ideas for caring for their employees was going to be a hard one. What Charles and I did not want was media madness. The selling of Kusta'ma Kare had to be done privately without any attention drawn from the media and outside bidders. I could have a meeting with the board members first, and with all our heads together come up with a plan of action to sell. What we did not want to do was spend another ten years trying to achieve that goal.

It was Kusta'ma Kare's ten-year anniversary. Jason called and announced that he would be flying into New York, and then to the island. We insisted that he stay at the villa, but Jason only stated that he had reservations in New York. Nonsense, I said, I will have the limousine pick you up at the hotel, and you can come into the island by company jet.

"Thank you, Linda, I will see you and Dad in a few days. I want to get one night's good rest before another flight. I have something to tell you."

Charles had been waiting looking out off the balcony for an hour. He did not like the "I've got something to tell you" news from Jason. When the jet did land, Charles saw the pilot first, the coach assistant, Jason, and then someone he did not know come down the flight stairs. Charles called back to me, "Linda, did Jason mention that he was bringing guests?"

Jason had been away at school now for over six years; he had more alphabets behind his name for business, management, and corporate law. Jason, I believe, was born to succeed and took advantage of his gift to retain information once seen or heard. Jason in short was a genius; we just had no idea what career path he would apply his genius mind to.

Kusta'ma Kare's anniversary celebration was the day after tomorrow so Charles and I would get plenty time to spend with Jason and his mystery guest. That same night at the dinner table, the mystery guest was no longer a mystery guest. Right before dinner, Jason stood to make a toast. "Dad, Linda, I would like to present my wife, Janelle Louise Edwards." Janelle was breathtakingly beautiful and I believed a perfect match for Jason. The four of us talked for hours. Janelle was from France but had lived stateside most of her life until she went back to school and met Jason where they dated only once and knew it was true love. She had just as many or more degrees behind her name as Jason for advertising, marketing, and business management. The more I talked to Janelle and listened to her outlook in life, the more she reminded me of myself. I liked her immediately and now know why Jason married her.

That night, Charles said, "Linda, I always knew Jason would turn out okay, but this is amazing." Charles and I spoke of other things that would be announced at the celebration, and then he said, "Linda, are you thinking what I'm thinking?" I said, "Yes, we can only ask."

Guest came from all over the world, heads of state, members of congress, senators, mayors, it turned out to be a gala event the held worldwide coverage. Three major networks covered the event.

After two days or resting, swimming, and eating, Charles and I asked Jason and Janelle for lunch on the balcony.

"Jason," Charles said, "Linda and I are ready to turn over Kusta'ma Kare, but we have been at a dilemma. Linda and I talked last night, and I know Kusta'ma Kare is a huge responsibility, but we were wondering if we could sign it over to you for a wedding gift."

Jason dropped the glass that he was drinking from. Later that night, I shared with Jason and Janelle "The Call," the vision and the journey. Jason and Janelle stayed three weeks while all necessary papers were signed and they took over Charles's old residence on the island. Ciania had someone new to protect, Janelle. Bernard, Barbara, and the team made it a smooth transition. Charles and I stayed on as advisors of Kusta'ma Kare for six months. Jason and Janelle would do well. They started off a lot smarter than I did. I hope they don't change the name. I'm kind of fond of Kusta'ma Kare, although no one ever knew what it really meant but I. Simple put Kusta'ma Kare means to take care, of oneself and others. Well, it was a journey, and now I guess I will have to read in the *Wall Street Journal* Kusta'ma Kare the after math.

Current day . . . Still on the balcony looking off in the distance thinking how wonderful and totally complete my life is.

Yes, the eerie feeling crawling up my spine had all but disappeared. My mind and I are finally at peace and sharing the same time and space. I did leave my mark in life, and not on life. I was destined for great things and great amounts of money. As memory faded of days past, I heard the clanging of keys on the kitchen counter and Charles calling up to me saying, "Honey, I'm home."

Who says that you can't have it all!